WILLIAM

WILLIAM

Fred Fox

FIRST EDITION

ISBNs:
Paperback: 978-1-80541-038-6
eBook: 978-1-80541-039-3

Introduction

Out of financial desperation, Mr Nice Guy finds hidden talents and a soul mate with identical thinking. Both believe strongly in the importance of their dictum "NEEDS MUST." This unity and combined strength of the mind is a path to success. They dispatch any problems arising with similar professional, decisive action, whether this involves evasion, trapping or murder. But can it work forever?

IF IT ENDS, WHAT IS LEFT?

Contents

Coping with debt and adversity changing to abundance through friendship and loyalty.

Also, with the ability to meet fire with fire... Trapping, evasion and murder, with more of the same.

Love and understanding are unquestionably first choice, but NEEDS MUST.

Dedication

Cannabis has many good and bad qualities, according to whose hands it is in. From a desperate need to casual recreational use, it can also be used as a tool for evil money-making, leading to envy and greed.

Yet there is an undeniable multi-medicinal benefit from its sensible, hopefully legal, use.

It is about time it was legalised, taking it out of the hands of criminals and their sordid underworld. We would still have to face the issue of addiction, but it would be better to deal with that than a larger problem of enormous debts, coupled with criminality on top of addiction.

I hope this story helps show how different people are affected. A normal, decent, understanding human being can gradually get drawn in to a horrific degree. Whereas there is no excuse, the problem would not have existed if the growing and use of cannabis were legalised.

Back in the real world, the same analogies exist around the horrors of the addict and criminal advantage takers versus health advantages and freedom.

The positive advantages completely outweigh the disadvantages, I believe, as do many others.

LEGALISE CANNABIS

Chapter 1

William sat, as usual, by the workshop door and the phone that lately only seemed to ring with bad or useless news ... "We are in a recession," "Are you busy?" "Have you anything booked in?" Those types of calls, plus numerous sales ones.

'I would try to get a job, but it's been so long, I am probably unemployable!' thought William. And anyway, the type of job around here would not give him and his family anywhere near what they were used to or needed ...

There is nothing booked in for next week, and if nothing turns up soon, he will have to let the "boys" go. The "boys" are two old, unadventurous men reliant on small wages and even smaller workloads. Goodness knows what they were doing today, with no jobs and a tidy workshop.

As though suddenly inspired, William thought, 'I will go to the bank!'

What difference that would make, he could only imagine, but it would be someone to talk to … "It's good to talk," he had heard somewhere!!!

Just then, a car came round the corner and stopped. William strode out with his smiling, welcoming, car-side manner only to find it was a car they had already worked on recently for a now-displeased owner.

As usual, William's thoughts were, 'I hope this ex-customer will get unfriendly and demanding.' That would give William a chance to fall out with him, argue and advise the man in motor trade language to "Fuck off." The opposite and less favourable situation would be if this man turned out to be friendly and understanding. It would then become impossible not to (reluctantly) say, "OK, we will have another go at repairing it, but I can't promise much as we are up to our eyes in work right now."

Unfortunately, the man took the inconvenient option, and William found himself agreeing to have another go at it: more expense, more materials.

The next morning, William met with Mr Knox at the bank.

"Good morning, William," greeted the manager with the fix-it face. "What can I do for you today?"

"Well, Mr Knox, business is bad. No work, little cash flow. I think I should sell everything."

Doubtlessly thinking of all the lovely bank charges they would be missing if he did sell to pay off the loans, Mr Knox came back with, "It was a good business and will be again. This recession will be over by Christmas."

"That is all very well for you to say, but if that's true, why send me demanding letters for repayment of loans that, in your words, have become 'hard borrowing'?" Then, not wanting to appear too sharp, William finished jokingly, "Anyway, you are a bank; you have lots of money, so why keep asking me to send you some?" He laughed. "As you say, Mr Knox, if the recession will be over by Christmas, perhaps it would be more helpful to take the pressure off and stop the demand till then."

"I don't know about that, William. It's not up to me; it's bank policy ... Do your best. Perhaps advertise!!!"

The weekend was here again. Wages were paid, but there was no more sign of work. Talking to the bank had been fruitless. The pub seemed the next option, which would mean talking and advertising. William was certainly not against a drink or two and, of course, the company of others. However, for the amount of trade he drummed up, he was spending quite a portion on drinks to impress or seduce likely customers. Like quicksand, the more you struggle, the more you sink, including financially.

It was on one of these occasions in The Star pub he found himself talking to a recent acquaintance, and the conversation turned to how to make money.

Dick, his new acquaintance, said, "Of course, you do know the quickest way to make money, don't you?"

Now William, although already aware he had disclosed more of his private situation than he liked, started to listen more carefully.

"Dope," Dick said.

He had William's attention. He inquired, "What? Growing? Or selling? Or what?"

"Growing is best, but you need cash to set up, and that's dangerous and easy to get. Selling is not so profitable, but not so punishable as long as it's small quantities."

The rest of the evening, regardless of the conversation, William's mind was fixed on the pros and cons of the cannabis trade. He gradually and casually managed to change the subject back around to drugs, asking what it would cost to set up to grow.

"It all depends," replied Dick, "on how big a set-up you want. You could earn a hundred grand a year if you spent twenty grand on a hydroponic system and good seed, a bit more if you had an aeroponic unit because it's quicker. Anyway, look it up on the internet. Everything's there; all advice, the kit, where to get it and prices."

"Wouldn't they be able to check you out and catch you through the internet?" William questioned. "It's not exactly private."

William had asked all the questions he dared without appearing too interested, or so he thought, and he changed the subject again. However, on the drive home, he thought of little else. His first thought was to borrow someone else's laptop to do his research on. It would have to be someone not closely associated with him or ever likely to be involved in growing anything untoward themselves; you could never be too careful.

Tomorrow, he would borrow a laptop from work on the pretence that his was out of order. He would erase anything he had googled when finished, and no one would be any wiser.

It took him two days locked in his office to complete and make his notes. There was a massive amount of information, and it was beginning to seem very complicated. He had sourced everything and priced it up. It was all a bit too much to take in in one go, but something needed to be done soon.

The weekend was again upon him; rugby would take up all Saturday, the wife and kids all Sunday, making Monday the big decision day.

On Saturday, apart from the actual playing time, his mind was full of ideas and plans. On Sunday, he did his best to entertain and appear to be attentive to the children, but his new project was taking him over.

On Monday, with a clear mind, he attacked the project. The shed at the end of the yard at work would be good and out of the way enough not to attract unwanted attention. He cleared it out, cut holes for extraction and laid extra electricity to it, all under the pretext of it being a new spray booth.

The extraction he fitted included filters to stop the easily recognisable smell that would inevitably be pumped out, keeping the proposed plants fresh with clean air.

As he went home that night, he called in at the pub and luckily found Dick inside. Casually getting around to the subject again, he pumped him for more information, details etc. The more details he got, the more he doubted his capabilities.

'Perhaps there is another way,' he was thinking, when all of a sudden, Dick provided him with an option.

"Of course," Dick said, "there are little gangs around that will pay well for a safe space to do this. They set it all up with all their stuff; you sit back and do nothing. It's less money but easier."

'That's for me,' William thought!

Naturally, the rest of the evening was spent thinking of the downsides ... Once in there, would you be able to get them out or get rid of them? What sort of a hold would they have? Once switched on, would it be possible to switch it off and move? Some of these people could be pretty evil ... The next thought line was, how long before a payday? He could not see it marrying up somehow.

Dick had a contact who knew people who did this and would ring on his behalf. Dick was becoming more of a confidante than William had originally wanted, but it seemed the only hope, and he grasped it.

A few days later, a Turkish man appeared at the garage – a runner for the main gang – to arrange everything.

William's first question was, "When do I get paid?" This was his main concern.

"As soon as the first crop's harvested," was the Turk's reply. "About three months."

Unfortunately, long before the three months would be up, William would have invested all he had and be behind with payments on his business loans with still little or no sign of business getting any better ...

"No," William decided. Too many people in the know would be a bad idea. To trust more than one person would be dangerous. Just he and his friend Dick was more than enough: William to quietly do all the growing, etc., and Dick to sell it.

Every day, William read details and spent three or four hours fitting the shed with the necessary equipment. He also spent one day a week travelling as far out of the area as possible to different suppliers for lights, nutrients, etc., without being recognised. Three weeks of this, and the grow room was ready.

It was time to chat with Dick again, who was his helpful self as usual. As William had hoped, he offered to sell any produce to a dealer as often as William wanted; that way, he would only be involved in growing and have nothing to do with selling. He was quick to say this could all be done without the buyer knowing where it was being produced. Oh yes, Dick assured him that would be the way: he would be the only link to both, neither aware of the other.

'Great!' thought William, 'I will order the seeds.'

These duly arrived and were soon small, fast-growing plants. William had done his home-work well, and the environment was perfect in this purpose-built shed. In another two weeks, they would be big enough to take cuttings from. Five days later, these had rooted, and very soon, there were three hundred well-rooted plants ready under rows of high-powered grow lamps for 16 hours a day and darkness for the other 8 hours. They were all automatically watered with nutrients three times a day for a minute each time. Next, the lighting pattern needed to be changed to imitate winter: light on for 11 hours and off for 13. The plants, now convinced winter had come, would quickly fruit, in other words, grow nice large buds of cannabis. From now on, a whole year's cycle would arrive, then fruit and go every nine weeks in the shed. It would be harvested, dried, packed and sold one week later, making the bank and William happier.

All went well, and Dick, a man of his word, arrived to collect.

"Right," he said, "I will take it to the buyer; he will check the quality and offer a price."

"Thanks, Dick. Let me know as soon as possible how you get on." William was congratulating himself on taking the chance and producing quickly; it now looked as though he would have a payday in time to ward off other problems.

Two days later, Dick came back with his report. "Yes, it was OK. Not great, but the buyer will offer two thousand pounds per kilo."

William had expected more, but for the first crop, fair enough. Anyway, Dick had said if the quality got better, it could possibly sell for three thousand ... One other thing: Dick would need five hundred to deliver each batch as it was too dangerous to do it for nothing.

William's first thought was, 'The profit's getting less and less. But OK,' he supposed, 'beggars can't be choosers.' He decided to get what he could and then make changes later when and if possible.

This situation continued in a similar fashion for the rest of the year, and William never got any more for a batch. In fact, the buyer was complaining he was not able to sell it as well as he had, and it was now worth less than originally agreed. The shed was producing as much as possible, and there was no room for more plants. More production could help, but where? And anyway, Dick and this buyer were not going to be forthcoming with any more money. Dick also added that the buyer said he was not getting paid as quickly as he should and was therefore going to be behind with payments to William: not good news.

William was not the calmest nor most trusting of men at the best of times. Much more of this type of news could push him to drastic or violent action, but for now, he was managing to hide his emotions.

In an effort not to rock the boat, he would work out an answer. On the one hand, the shed was too small, and on the other, the buyer could not be trusted. Dick, it seemed, was creaming off more than he made out, so either way, a change was needed.

William had an idea. Without Dick and co knowing, he would buy a freezer lorry that was made for delivering frozen food. They are, of course, insulated and large enough to grow and fruit in. He would just need more rooted cuttings from the shed. That would be easy enough, and then the container could be backed up out of sight and linked to an electric source for the heating lamps. In case of emergency, the whole thing could be driven away undetected by anyone, including Dick. William had already decided to travel at least three hundred miles to another town to find a buyer. Perhaps he could achieve a more sensible financial state then. Well, he would know in around three months, so the sooner he started, the better.

Chapter 2

William was pushing Dick for the outstanding money as much as he could, the excuse being he soon would not be able to produce as he had without cash.

Dick's answer was, "Do what you can, and I will get what I can. I can't get them to pay any more for it!!!!"

"No, but it's getting harder to convince the wife that I am not earning enough from my legitimate car repairs when she can tell I have been spending more than usual just by looking at the bank statements. If things don't improve, she'll suspect me of having an affair – an expensive one at that."

She had been given enough reason to believe that in the past, and William was sure she would not forgive him again, no way. "Please, get me my money," he pleaded. "I am definitely going to have to spend more time at home with the family from now on ..." William thought that ought to be enough of an excuse to be away from work and the grow shed without Dick knowing about the lorry grow unit or his search for another better buyer.

William parked the lorry on the waste ground alongside other vehicles. On most evenings, he took tools and equipment and started work, fitting it out like the shed. If anyone asked, it was just having general repairs carried out when he had time. This was going well and twice as fast as the shed had because he knew where everything needed to go this time, including the new large electric fuse box and wiring. He backed it into his yard behind the grow shed and connected it all up to the free supply. He would use it in conjunction with the shed for now until another more secret site could be found or arranged.

The remaining task was the most important one: to find a reliable, intelligent contact – someone who would not talk unnecessarily and, at the same time, was appreciative of extra cash. There were plenty of the other types – users or addicts to drink and cannabis, or just too talkative – all willing to work for payment. But besides them being dangerous, you could never know who their friends were or who they would talk or brag to. The old adage came to mind, "If you lie down with dogs, you get up with fleas!!!" So, in business, be careful who you get into bed with.

William thought a good place to start would be the Forest of Dean as it has a lot of small farms and struggling farmers, all usefully private and separated from one another, away from prying eyes. The arrival of a lorry or any old vehicle there would not be unusual. In fact, it was quite a common occurrence, the barns being rented out cheaply and useful for storage or workshops. So, a few days in the Forest it would be; a careful few days, though. William could not afford to show his hand too soon for fear of approaching the wrong man. First, a quiet pint here and there and a casual chat with a lot of research.

Two days of this had uncovered possibilities, but before choosing and exposing his idea, more contact and personal chats were necessary. William made his decision. Arthur, a man now living on his own, was of an age. He had worked a very small farm with his wife all their married life, just keeping their heads above water by doing a bit of general buying and selling furniture.

Unfortunately, she had died of cancer a year or so ago now, and Arthur was no longer interested in anything they had done before. He had become very bitter. William had seen in him, amongst all else, a large sense of loyalty and the need for a cause. They met up several more times for general explanations, which gave them both a chance to open up in shows of trust.

There was a bond and a purpose for Arthur, and it was time to get started.

"Arthur, we will need access to electricity," William explained. "If I rent that little shed at the back end of the house, I can connect to the back of your old fuse box. It won't alter your consumption at all, and should it ever be found, then you know nothing about it, the excuse being that you can show the area is rented to me. At the same time as paying you rent, as agreed, I can supply you with a free connection to electric power as well. From now on, you can tell anyone you are renting that area to me for repairs; that way, they will not be surprised when I turn up."

Feeling it was a good and safe thing to agree to, Arthur came back with a further suggestion. "How about you pay me a bit extra to look after things in your absence, such as water and nutrient levels? I am happy to do that and would be keen to learn."

'Great!' William thought, as that was just what was needed. "Later this week," he said, "I will drive over, fix the electrics and get started. I can pay you the first six months' rent now. What do you think?"

"OK," Arthur said. He was happy with regular rent, free electricity and a learning curve on growing; all this, at no danger to him.

William soon drove over and fixed the wiring, and Arthur drove him back. The following weekend, William would arrive with everything to get the process started, which was an opportunity to give Arthur his first lesson. This suited Arthur as he was beginning to get his interest in life back and a new purpose.

Meanwhile, back at work and the shed, the struggle with Dick and the buyer over the cash owing had got no easier. They knew they had the upper hand and were never going to pay more than necessary, that being just enough to ensure another batch. The struggle went on. William spoke every other day on the phone, albeit cryptically, to an enthusiastic Arthur.

Arthur was sure he had come up with a buyer, a cousin who was used to selling whenever he had been able to buy any bud before.

"OK," William had agreed, but only on the understanding that cousin Ted never knew where it originated from and just that Arthur was managing to buy at a reasonable price fairly locally. With this agreed, William told Arthur to proceed and trusted him to sort out beneficial prices. This was another huge step forward, and now William needed to meet up with Dick. The problem remained that William had to proceed carefully to finish with Dick. He and the buyer could be problematic as, no doubt, they would cause trouble under these circumstances. All that could be safely done now was to ask for payments to be bought up to date while slowing the amount of cannabis available to them. After all, without them knowing, William had got an outlet for any excess and was much more certain to get the money for it.

This was a business where it could be fatal to upset anyone and could only be run on total trust. The only other way out would be to close down completely and remove all equipment overnight, including tell-tale electric connections. It might, at some time, come to that, but first, it would be good to earn the initial set-up and equipment costs, and that could not happen without an income.

"Dick," said William, "I am not going to be able to go on without proper payment. It's very dangerous should I get caught anyway, so it's pointless while earning so little."

Dick had all the answers all ready for himself or the buyer. William had to take Dick's word as he had never known who the buyer was and quite honestly did not want to. The reasons Dick had ready were, "It's not selling very well, and the buyer can get it cheaper elsewhere," and "His clients have not paid him yet."

"That's his problem, not mine," said William. "If he or you want something, then you pay for it first – I have to! Last week he wanted me to go and buy different seeds. Sort it out, Dick, or I will dismantle it all."

The problem was he was pretty sure the buyer and Dick knew he couldn't, under normal circumstances, stop for at least a year or two to recover his outlay. So, regardless of his threats, the situation remained the same. They had the upper hand and had no intention of paying one penny more than necessary.

Which of these two was the fly in the ointment? Or was it both? He did not know but would put his mind to it – he must devise a way of testing. Perhaps it was all Dick, and there was no buyer all along. But, before he could decide what to do, he had to find out.

This weekend would be spent with the wife and children. It was school sports day and time he flew the family flag with no distractions. There were all the normal, "Hello, William, how are you? Good to see you and the wife," from various other couples, along with an "I gather my kids are friendly with yours. You must come over for the day sometime with them."

"Yes," William would reply, and again, several times, "We must arrange something," "I will ring you," or "Ring me; it will be good to hear from you," "Any time." Then he moved smartly on smiling, probably more because he was escaping than if he had a happy meeting. William was not keen on getting tied down with definite dates or appointments.

His smile changed to a quizzical one as he had just caught sight of Dick. Strangely, he did not know if Dick was married or had children.

William still had no clue as he seemed to be with another man and then sometimes a woman, so he could actually be with either. This was not his first concern, but he wondered if the other man was the buyer. There was no definite reason to think this either way, but he could be. Just as William had spotted them, they seemed aware of him. A couple of times, they had taken turns to look casually across at William, each time pretending not to see him. William could well imagine the conversation Dick was having with his companion.

"Don't look now, but that's William over there."

"Where? Oh, I see; the one in the black jacket?"

"Yes, with the fair hair and blue jeans."

"Yes, I see. Has he seen us?"

"Don't think so. Don't let him catch you looking. He might jump to conclusions about who you are, and we don't want that do we?"

The two groups managed to keep well apart without showing any obvious signs of deliberately avoiding each other. However, at the same time, William had dispatched his wife to take a surreptitious photo of Dick and his friend. She did it without question; she was used to his ways and just thought it was to do with his work. William would now get another third party to find who the man actually was and where he was from. At this moment, he had no idea how he could use this information, but he was sure it would be useful sooner or later.

William planned to stay at his workshop and shed for most of the next two weeks, knowing he would be needed by Arthur. A few days after that, it would be approaching harvest time at the lorry for this new crop. He had to show Arthur what to do and how to tell when it was ready. He was a willing and fast learner but still needed to be shown the ropes at the important stages. Harvesting was one, then trimming and hanging to dry. To kill two birds with one stone, William would take cuttings from the shed to plant as the new crop in the lorry as soon as they had cut down the crop there for harvesting. After two days, harvesting was finished, the next crop was planted, and William returned to work unnoticed.

Two weeks later, he went back to Arthur for the final trimming, weighing and packaging. The final teaching went well, and Arthur swore he could manage on his own most of the time. Well, at least this venture was going OK, and the next two weeks were vital: cropping, drying, trimming, shrink wrapping.

Chapter 3

From sports day onwards, William had been spending less time with his wife and family. Additionally, his business problems had increased. Therefore, it did not come as a surprise when he discovered his wife had moved out and was asking for a divorce. Although it affected him badly, he did not think, in all fairness, that he should get in her way. It seemed much fairer to go along with what she wanted. He had nothing better to offer her and had never been at one with her as a wife: a mistake made when young. As papers came, he signed; as demands came, he paid. There was no point in doing anything else, and besides that, the rest of his life was so full of problems and trauma. It hurt, but it would be another large thing not to have to worry about or try to work at.

William felt happy to let Arthur take it all to sell all in one go. Arthur saw to it and came back with the right money from his cousin, who, according to Arthur, was very pleased and could not wait for the next lot. William was now getting a little nervous. Everything had gone so well that he was half expecting Sod's law to kick in and for something to go wrong. He was not going to voice his fears in case it meant painting the devil on the wall, "Lest he should appear." For now, all was good, so he would stay quiet and keep his fingers crossed!! That is often easier said than done.

After a week of careful detective work, a name for Dick's mysterious friend had been provided: Andrew Bowls. Yet another link; a Pakistani, and possibly the biggest link in this particular chain. Whether the biggest or not, the Pakistani branch had a very bad reputation. No name was ever used, but a large number of people seemed to be aware of him.

This was exactly what William had not wanted. This was a big and dangerous chain and a reason for the lack of cash flow. To William, all of these links were grabbing a share, meaning there was little left for him. This also meant that any serious conflict with any link in the chain would end very badly. What to do about it? That was the problem – whatever he did would need very careful planning. Nothing could be changed very quickly without causing suspicion. He blamed Dick as he must have known the seriousness of the chain but cared little as long as he got his cut.

By now, Arthur was also experiencing similar problems with payments. It turned out that the cousin he was supplying had been turned and was supplying yet another link in the Pakistani chain with the violent reputation. This chain was not as long but nevertheless as dangerous. There had to be a way out of this situation.

First, William needed an honest and frank face-to-face conversation with Arthur to see what suited them both. The one good thing was no one other than Arthur and William knew where Arthur's cannabis farm was. If they did, there was no doubt it would not take the Pakistani links long to find it. At the moment, no one was concerned or even bothered to check. As long as they were all getting their greedy little paws on their share, they would not want the trouble: just money for nothing or very little. Either way, by now, the belt and braces way of surviving for William was kicking in again. He never drove anywhere without carefully watching his rearview mirror.

Even then, he doubled back or rerouted his journeys, never going directly to or from anywhere. He messaged Arthur and arranged to meet him in secret a long way from his farm. At this meeting, they must come to a mutually agreeable decision. William hoped Arthur would turn out to be as strong-minded as him and was not the type to roll over and give in. Any sign of weakness and they would be at the mercy of the big links forever. This type of business was successfully built on secrecy and fear: each chain in fear of the next. Tomorrow's meeting was to be decisive and most important. Before they met, William had twelve hours thinking through the pros and cons of various actions and little if no sleep.

"I am sorry to have got you into this situation," William said. "If I had known we would have had these problems, I would not have got you into it. I will understand perfectly if you want me to disconnect everything before anyone is any the wiser."

Arthur stood silent for a moment and then said, "William, it's not your fault. Besides, it gave me a purpose in life – the purpose I needed to get me through. When my wife died, my life ended too. I wanted nothing. I was at the end when you came along and got me back from the brink. I am back living again, and I've learnt a lot. It might be a bit rough from now on, but I am alive and up for a fight. In fact, I'm looking forward to it; I just hope you are too, William. Let's not be beaten."

"Great," was William's reply. "We have given these sly bastards too much respect already. Why? I don't know. To avoid trouble, I suppose, but trouble or not, it's time to show them who is who. Let's plan this carefully. For a start, we act the same hard done by innocents until the trap is shut. The first thing is that whatever we do cannot be traced back to us – that allows for anything goes."

Arthur agreed.

"Starting today, we grow and harvest madly but don't supply to anyone. Just squirrel it away somewhere safe, well away from here. I am going to tell Dick that I am developing the shed to be twice the size. That will give us extra time. Then, by the time they are curious, we will have stripped out all incriminating equipment and wiring, so whatever happens, there will be no comeback there. The lorry, the same. As soon as the last crop is harvested, we deconstruct the inside, drive it off and use it for drying and storage again, well away from here. Then, when we are ready, bring it back with just empty boxes in it.

"Next, Arthur, we must decide who we catch in the trap. The one card we still have that we can be sure of is that you can guarantee none of these sly minions trust one another. It's human nature in this business to distrust. We need to get the top man to distrust one or two of his assistants enough so that he has to check things out person-ally. I am then going to be his new best friend. What do you think, Arthur?"

"Sounds dangerous, but it could work."

"Let's get on with the first part of this plan and produce the maximum in both places."

This they did, and over the next three months, they packaged and stored everything possible. Dick was beginning to make unhappy noises. The links above and the head man, Raj, were get-ting anxious about the lack of deliveries. Raj had been temporarily calmed with the tale that there was a much larger delivery on the way. Time was approaching fast for the final act, but it could not be rushed. Once the distrust button had been pressed, the plan had to move on quickly before anyone had time to get nosy.

William boldly knocked on Raj's door. He was shocked to discover that William knew where he lived and who he was. Raj was even more perturbed to be told his home had been pointed out by Dick and Andrew when William had delivered the bumper crop to them two weeks ago. William then pointed out he had come to see Raj because he had not been paid for it. Raj immediately reacted how William wanted him to.

"What are they up to?" he screamed. "We have had nothing from you or them for months."

William tried to answer, saying, "Best to see for yourself, to be sure. I know where we delivered it to. I could take you there, then they can't argue. You might be getting ripped off, like me. Or Raj, do nothing for a while – don't frighten them off. I will check that it's still there. Say nothing to them. By offering to deliver a few more kilos, if they say nothing by midweek, I will take you to see for yourself. Then you will know what to do without making a mistake. I only want a regular payment. Please. Then I will always look after your interests."

Raj was seething but agreed.

William just hoped Raj could keep calm until he took him to the checkpoint lorry.

William rushed back to Arthur. "It's all set. We have a few days to empty the lorry other than some packing boxes. And Arthur, you do know that once the trap is sprung, we can never stop it. It's a one-off final solution; no half-measure will do. If not completed, all hell will be unleashed, and a lot of it will fall on us."

"William, as you have always said, if something needs to be done, then it must be done, no matter what."

"OK, Arthur, on with the show. The lorry is empty. We will park it on the waste ground behind Dick's house. As soon as it is dark, I will bring Raj around. Arthur, can you sit near but out of sight – in case need you?"

Everything was in place early, and of course, it would be a long, anxious afternoon wait. Dusk arrived, and the unlit wasteland was suitably dark – good for this operation. William collected a still agitated Raj and drove to the lorry. On the way, he pointed out Dick's house, helpfully close to the lorry.

"Oh, yes," Raj remarked. "Very handy for Dick."

"Raj, you see that lorry over there? That's where they store stuff, the dope that is all supposed to go to you. I won't park too close in case someone is watching. Then we can approach it from the side, again, without being seen."

"Good idea, William. I am glad you are calm and careful – it saves a lot of fuss."

William handed Raj a torch. "You will need this," he told him, "but don't switch it on until you are in. When you are out again, we will visit Dick and get this stuff collected, so be careful not to give anyone a chance to run and hide."

Raj seized the torch and soon jumped into the back. William gladly and smartly slammed the door shut and locked it. This was a freezer airtight lorry body with a thick insulated body: soundproof and with no way out.

Arthur was soon at William's side. "Are you OK?"

"Yes, and you, Arthur?"

"I know it's drastic, but this snake and his little gang was always going to be dangerous and needed its head cut off. Without Raj, this snake is useless. Arthur, are you still happy to drive the lorry off to the scrap yard quarry and dump it? Don't forget your gloves. I will pick you up."

The lorry was soon at its final resting place, parked insignificantly at the end of the quarry where other old wrecks were left. No one would be interested. The most likely thing to happen would be that after a year or so, they might set fire to them and bury them where they had been dumped. In the meantime, if anything of Raj came to light, they would more than likely jump to the convenient conclusion – "Must have been an illegal immigrant." No one was going to miss Raj – a man who lived alone and only went out on criminal business. His assistants would be concerned that they might disappear as well, and that was more than enough to worry about.

"OK, Arthur, on to the next stage. Are you ready?"

"Yes. I will go back to the farm and visit the links in the gang on my end while you see to Dick and Andrew. Then we can meet up later in the week to compare notes. OK, partner?"

"Ideal, partner."

Chapter 4

It was taking Dick and Andrew some time to try to understand what was going on, especially with the disappearance of Raj. It was time for William to step in and help them to come to the conclusions he needed them to.

The first seeds of thought were sown by William in Dick's mind when he walked up to Dick and said, "Hey, Dick, have you met any of this London mob yet? What is Raj doing about them? They cleared everything I had with big warnings. Took all my equipment as well, so I am out of business as of now ... If you see any of them, I strongly advise you not to argue with them!!" 'That should do the trick,' thought William. 'Now their vivid imaginations will run wild.'

Dick's first response was, "Raj has disappeared. We have been trying to contact him. He must have taken his eye off the ball. Just shows you can't trust anyone."

William guessed it was time to feed them a bit more information, even though false, and then leave them to think themselves into panic and fear!!

"I was walking to my car yesterday," he said, "when a car pulled up by me. Two men got out and called my name. Two more stayed in it. They said, 'Raj is gone! We want no opposition.' So you and the others – I presumed he meant you and Andrew – will be left alone as long as we all mind our own business and don't start anything in opposition to them. They said they would be watching us, to make sure and, if in future they thought we could help them, they would contact us. Well, I believe them – they cleared my workshop out. Now, I prefer they never need me. I am out. You can make your own minds up."

William felt quietly confident he had convinced Dick that this was what had occurred and that he was speaking the wise truth. The fear of disappearing as Raj had done was firmly planted in their minds, meaning they would make the right decisions.

William hoped Arthur was having the same success. It was time for them to meet up again.

The next day, William drove to meet up with Arthur. They had both been doing a lot of thinking and had pretty well come to the same conclusions.

"We have a lot of equipment, William," Arthur stated, "and it would be difficult to dump. It would be easy enough to drive away from here and sell the bags of produce, and we do need to get completely out of this business. So far, we have been lucky, but it would only take a couple of coincidences before our past would be suspected or worked out. And although there is no London mob here or moving in, it might not be long before one does. We don't want to be caught holding the wrong end of any stick."

"OK, Arthur. I totally agree, and I think I have a suitable answer. Firstly, the equipment. If carefully advertised in small units, I am sure there are thousands of people suffering health-wise and in desperate need of medical cannabis. It might take years to find enough people to take on growing small units medically for themselves and friends, but it's worth a try for a good cause."

"Brilliant, William. I never really spoke much about my wife, but it would have made her life so much more bearable and comfortable. After the last two years or three years, I wish I had known then what I know now ... Also, William, I am still in touch with the support groups, and I know a large number of people who went were of one mind. They wish they had had the know-how and equipment to produce and help their struggling partners and families."

"Well, there you go, Arthur, my friend. Do it. You have enough technology and equipment to set up dozens, if not hundreds, of little units and even offer sample goods to seduce people to give it a try. With all that and all the contacts you have, I am sure they would be eternally grateful. You needed a purpose, Arthur, you now can have the best of purposes, and I am proud to know you. Go for it."

"William, I love the idea, but what about you?"

"Well, at the moment, I need nothing. I have enough money to get me out of debt. I will go back to the motor trade and find work. It'll be hard for a while, but sooner or later, the gypsy in me will need to move on to pastures and experiences new. The one and biggest need I will always want is your friendship, so whatever happens, stay in touch."

"OK, William. I need that as well. We meet or talk once or twice a month, and this is the second time you have given me a purpose. I will never forget it. How us two mentally-hardened men became one, I will never know, but I'm very grateful we did. Now we both hope medicinal cannabis will become legalised soon. Just remember, we did what we had to do. 'NEEDS MUST,' and luckily, we were man enough to do it."

The next three months went by boringly. Business was poor, as usual, but enough to get by and pay the bills. All very well, but it was such a vast contrast to the fast-moving life of the last year. William often sat quietly contemplating the past, looking at the passers-by, thinking, 'I could do a Raj to any of you' – in other words, kill or at least plot their death or downfall. He had changed, and he knew it. He had a calm feeling of superiority over all around him. 'Whatever, whenever, I can deal with it, no panic,' he thought. He had noticed several new faces around town and wondered why they were there. They seemed to be loitering, possibly up to no good. 'So what?' he thought.

However, it was no great surprise when, one evening in his workshops, four of these strangers entered and placed themselves around.

"William, we need to talk to you," the one who appeared to be the leader said. "We have spoken to all sorts of people in our search for our associate Raj and most of the information has led to you. So here we are, William, and we won't leave without an answer. What happened to Raj?? We know you have the answers; we have watched you for some time. You don't meet anyone or do anything out of the ordinary; you just work in this poxy garage, and that is not normal. It's time to talk. Now or never."

Still full of calm, William replied cheekily, "You gave me a choice, so never!"

Losing patience, the inquisitor said, "That was not a choice, dick head – it was a live or die."

"Either way, I don't know, so do your worst, arsehole," William said. He grabbed a wrench off the bench and swung it at the nearest one, catching him on the shoulder, but not before he felt a sharp bang in the back. He was now swinging furiously, but this was a well-practised gang. He was stabbed again and again without being able to inflict much damage on them.

For the moment, they were bleeding him but leaving him alive long enough to get their answers. He was feeling weaker all the time but would never give in. He rolled onto his back, grinned at the ringleader and tried a final ruse. "You don't know the trouble you are in now. Good luck, you will need it. Ha ha ha ha," his false laugh rang out.

Then, as if on cue, there was a bang, and a man with a gun was standing in the doorway. "Are ye OK, Wulliam?" the man said in a broad Scottish accent. The accent did not normally go with the man holding the gun, but William guessed why.

"Yes, Jock. Better now you are here. Are the others keeping watch?"

"Aye, all under control, mun. What do you want us to do with these?"

"They want to talk to Raj."

"OK, which one does the talking?"

William pointed to the ringleader. "That one," he said, then whispered, "the snake's head" and winked.

"Well, he shall go to him then."

They tied and gagged all four of them and loaded them into the transit van after relinquishing their phones and personal things. They drove off, and after twenty miles or so, in a deserted area, they pulled three out, still bound, gagged and now blindfolded. They tied them to a tree.

"We will be back with your boss in an hour after he speaks to Raj, so behave yourselves."

They drove off to the quarry with a new snake's head. Posing as Jock, Arthur and William were reading each other's minds. Once in the quarry, it was night. They were alone and soon found the old freezer lorry. They quickly incarcerated the new snake's head (gangster) without much trouble, along with Raj. They relocked the door and covered their tracks back to the van.

Ten miles down the road, they stopped for a chat. "What now, Arthur? You saved my arse yet again!"

"Well, William, I had watched them gathering around you for a few days. They never noticed me, so I went and bought a gun. Always wanted one. I guessed they would make a move soon, but not as soon as they did. I had only just left the gun shop; they caught me napping. Where next? The hospital?"

"Yes, I think so. At a guess, I think we will have a week at the most to arrange things; then,

I will move on. I need a change, anyway. What about you, Arthur?"

"Me, the same. I know I do not have to move, and no one knows of me, but I also need a change, so I will tie up all my loose ends ready for a change."

"OK, as long as you are sure. I have a few ideas for me. First, the hospital, then rent out the garage. Pack everything necessary, and then one week tonight, we leave. Don't forget your passport."

"Right, one week tonight, then. I am looking forward to it a lot."

"Me too, Arthur. We were stagnating."

William gave a false name at the hospital in the next town, where he was admitted for two days. Then he went to the bank for cash and set up a rental agreement for the next mechanic to pay in. He then drove past the area where they had left the three men tied up. They were long gone, but it would take them a week or so to get themselves together to do anything. William bought a train ticket to Glasgow, making sure as many people as possible saw him struggling with his luggage boarding the train to Scotland. After all, his accomplice was Jock, so he must surely come from Scotland! That would be a good but false lead. Two towns further up the track, he quietly got off and went out to the waiting car with Arthur at the wheel.

"All done, pal?" William asked as he got in.

"Yes, all ready, William."

"No need for that awful Scottish accent now, then," he said, laughing.

"No, but I will keep it around just in case we need it in the future. After all, you always keep your Welsh one. Where to now, then, William?"

"I thought South of France and a business in the sun – what do you fancy?"

"I'm easily led by you, William, so lead on," Arthur replied.

"OK, so we head to Felixstowe to the Chunnel; three hours from now, we will be in France, heading south towards Toulouse," William instructed.

Chapter 5

Once in France, halfway into their journey, they stopped at a bed and breakfast. Both slept well and ate well; they thanked and paid their host. They asked the best way to Bordeaux, which was, in fact, the opposite direction to their intended destination, but caution had become second nature to them at all times.

Two or three hours later, they were at the foot of the Pyrenees mountains, where they would spend a few days as tourists. They intended to learn all they could about the area in order to find an appropriate property for business, which meant something out of sight and with plenty of out-buildings. As it happened, in this area, there were plenty, and they were cheap. They soon decided on one. The next decision was: what business to start? They had talked a lot in the car on the way down and decided on a front business of digging machines for hire, with or without a driver, or possibly a garage and mechanic. There was plenty of room here. Meanwhile, hidden away in the house would be the old favourite, cannabis. It was all falling into place, and with their experience, it would be constructed quickly. Once built and connected up to automatic lights and water, they would have time for socialising and networking. Of course, they still had to develop the front business, nothing too fancy at first – the money-making one inside was most important.

The first job now would be to find some possible outlets for their produce, but not too close: two hundred kilometres away in any direction would be ideal. Before the week was out, they had found two contacts willing to buy everything grown and at a sensible price. That suited everyone, as neither William nor Arthur would ever become drug sellers. A deal was struck, and William would phone the day of delivery with a delivery point for them to collect from. This would be a different place every time, and of course, cash only on collection or no deal.

"All set then, Arthur."

"Yes, all set, but one thought. How long before we are bored? It's all going too easily."

"Let's give it a month, and we could go back for a week or so. We only need to set the timers and nutrients tanks and, of course, lock everything up securely. Then we can fly home and see if I can get stabbed around a bit again for excitement, ha ha, 'Jock.' I will fly to Scotland and venture south from there, in case someone is watching. 'Belt and braces' as usual – separate cars. Right, I will organise some tickets. We need a break, or rather, the opposite of a break: an adrenaline buzz!!"

"I can't wait! It's great to be back together."

"Well, yes, that reminds me, Arthur. One other problem. How are you nowadays about female company? I would not want to suggest you go against your feelings for your wife, but we both need to be seen doing some romancing, or we will be the talk of the town."

"I had not thought of that, William; you think of everything. And in answer to your query, no problem. It's time to move on. I have wonderful memories, and no doubt always will have, but she would understand. I am glad you mentioned it. I was beginning to wonder about you, and it's a relief. I don't know about you, but I have seen a few nice possibilities in town already."

"Me too. I, er, er, I, er ..."

"You, er, what, William?"

"I, er, wondered if you fancied a ride into town for a beer or something now?"

"Yes, especially for the something else. Perhaps check things out. Oh shit, you know, let's just go and see!"

"Put some clean clothes on, too," William added.

"Yeah, let's at least try to make a good impression," Arthur

"On the pull then, Arthur."

They drove to the town square and joined the throng at what seemed to be the most popular bar, well, the busiest anyway.

"Take it slow, William. Check out the lay of the land and who is with who," Arthur joked. "We do not want to fight the local jealous men! Well, not yet, anyway."

"Unfortunately, Arthur, I don't see anything worth fighting over," William said.

"No, I think it is plan B for us today. Any port in a storm," he said, laughing.

"It's good to be out having a beer, anyway, and everyone is friendly. Another couple of beers, and we should go home to our lonely beds."

"Yes, I think so. Perhaps lunch here tomorrow and see what midday brings!"

Later, they drove home, unlocked and visited the grow rooms. The lights had automatically changed, and all had been watered successfully, but it was always worth checking.

"Bedtime, Arthur," William said.

"Yes."

The same in the morning. They checked everything, and all was OK, so they had a lazy breakfast and a chat.

"William, last night I got talking to an English mechanic who specialises in heavy machinery. I would like you to meet him later," Arthur explained. "If we agree, he could be an ideal frontman as a digger man and mechanic, and we could possibly use his name on any sign. The last thing we want is to attract attention to us, and that would also stop awkward questions from the tax man. I am pretty sure he is registered for tax. If he is any good, we could pay him well to keep the heat off us."

"We do need someone like that soon," William agreed. "Let's talk to him today if possible. That little piece of information was worth last night's trip and better than the quick fuck we originally went for."

"Yes, business first, fuck another day," Arthur said, laughing.

"Lunch in town and ask around. We will find him soon enough."

"Lock up, William; it's dinner time."

Luckily, the menu was in English as well as French, and the waitress also spoke English. The one thing they did not understand was how to cook meat. Whether medium or well done, there was no excuse for ruining the meat. All they could do was insist on "No blood."

"Arthur, the waitresses are better in the daytime," William said.

"And so are the diners."

"Night time, they are all big and boozy."

"It's a job to work out the ladies here. Several pairs of good lookers, but possibly gay, and the holidaymakers are almost certainly married and a lot of the others too. Oh well, no hurry."

"It's more important to find our mechanic, but I think that will have to be tonight. He doesn't seem to be here today. We have two choices: one, stay in town for the rest of the day to wait and see, or go back to work for a while and come back later and hope to catch him."

"Let us go back for a couple of hours or so, at least to check if all is well. Also, to see that no one is hanging around. Then we can come back for a beer tonight."

Everything was running smoothly, and they spent some time making sure. One thing was obvious, though; they really needed someone to keep an eye on the place whenever they were away. Therefore, tonight's job had become quite urgent. They spent an hour busying themselves and topping things up as necessary.

There was just time for a wash before going back into town.

"If we sit in the bar on the corner, we should see anyone who comes or goes and should be lucky."

One beer followed another, and they were beginning to wonder when, at last, he wandered in on his own. Arthur waved and called him over.

"Join us. I want you to meet my pal, William! I am sorry, I forgot your name. I am Arthur; this is William."

"Hello, I am Tom."

"Have you lived here long, Tom? But first, would you like a beer?"

"Yes, sure, and I have lived here five years. I came here with a wife, but things did not go well. We argued, and she went back, but now she says if I can find regular work, she will come and try again. It always comes down to financial security in the end. I make a living repairing trucks but mostly get stuck for premises to work in. We did some bed and breakfast, but I cannot do that on my own."

"Well, if you call by our yard tomorrow and look at what we have, I am sure we can work something suitable out. We often need a mechanic, and we have workshops suitable for anything. What do you think?"

"I think I will be there at 10 am tomorrow for a proper talk. Does that suit?"

"Perfect. Drink up. Let's celebrate in advance; I feel confident."

They all celebrated, but neither Arthur nor William drank too much – an inbuilt defence. Tom seemed to be the same – something that both boys noticed and liked. Without a word, William looked at Arthur and winked.

Tom arrived at 10 am on the dot the next morning, and they showed him around.

"Tom, we can pay you a retainer if you can work here, and then you can spend the rest of the time doing your own work. You run it as your own business in your name. That will save us getting involved in tax etc., and we would have someone to keep a watch on the place. What do you think of it so far?"

"OK, how much retainer?"

"Well, some weeks, we might need you to work half a day; other weeks, an hour or less. We will pay all overheads and give you 300 euros in cash every week regardless. The main thing for us, as I said, is we need someone to keep an eye on the place for us and keep our vehicles going. Hopefully, you will build your own business now you have premises for it. What do you think, Tom?"

"So far, so good. Let's give it a go."

"If all goes well, get your sign up so people can find you. Start Monday. Here is your first 300 euros. We would like you to move in as soon as possible; we need to go to the UK for a few days soon."

Tom started moving his tools etc., in straight away, ready for the Monday start.

"Good morning, Tom," William said on Monday morning. "Nothing much to do for us for a few days, but if possible, service the BMW next week – or before, if you have spare time. There is oil and everything you might want in the other shed. Anything else, let us know, and we will get it. Have a good day; we are going to town for a while."

They drove off feeling everything was safe and secure. The house was locked; no matter how nosey anyone was, there was nothing to be seen.

"Coffee and a talk then, William," Arthur said once they were settled in a café.

"Yes, next week you fly back to Bristol, Arthur. I will fly to Scotland and travel south – can't be too careful."

Chapter 6

Tom was settled in. Arthur had reached Bristol, and William was on the plane to Scotland, where he caught the train south to Birmingham and then Bristol. All this might have seemed a bit pointless, but as it happened, when William got to Bristol, he soon saw he was being watched. He acted suspiciously and pretended he had not seen the watchers. He threw the remains of his Scottish train ticket into a bin for someone to find, and they did!! He got a taxi to the village and called in at the pub for a drink and a chat. He did not stay long, just enough time to casually mention he was working in Scotland: a town called Gifford. He left and walked to the bus stop. Two stops further along, he got off, walked to the transport cafe, got a lift with a driver to the next town and called Arthur. Thirty minutes later, Arthur arrived to collect him.

"Were they watching, William?"

"Oh, yes, they were at the station. I pretended not to see them. I left my train ticket for them to find, and I also told our pub landlord I was working in Gifford, so they all know by now. Have you done all you needed to do here, Arthur?"

"Yes, all done. I passed the quarry, and nothing looks disturbed. So, what now?"

"I will take a taxi to the bank, check the garage rent is being paid and draw out some cash. By midday, I will be back on the Scottish train. You catch the train from Bristol, and we both get off at Birmingham. Watch my back to see if I am followed or not. I doubt if I am; they won't be expecting me to leave for a few days yet. If you do spot anyone, scratch your head, and I will get back on the train; otherwise, I'll take a taxi to Midland Airport. I have booked flights from there to Toulouse."

It all went easily. He was right; they were not expecting him to leave yet. The next day, if they checked, they would find he had left for Scotland on the train, but, in fact, they would be landing in Toulouse nearly home: mission accomplished.

"Well, William, we are going to be busy for the next week or so," Arthur said. "It is harvest time; that will take all week, and then we'll possibly need another two for drying, weighing and bagging. Then, it's the tricky part: delivery. I just hope they are not going to try anything silly."

"No, I am sure it will be okay. They need a safe, regular business as much as we do,"

"Yes, and we will be our usual careful belt and braces selves."

It was an eventless journey back. They drove into the yard where Tom was busying himself. The yard was looking tidy, and he was smiling. There was still no business sign up yet, but it was early days.

"I have good news. My wife is coming back; that's another good reason for me to make a real go of this."

"Any callers, Tom?" William asked.

"A few for me; otherwise, it's been quiet. I think my work is picking up, so if it's okay with you, I will get a sign put up this week."

"As soon as you like, Tom."

They unlocked the house and went into separate grow rooms.

"Wow, William, they have really grown!" Arthur called through to William. "This room is a mass of large bud; we can start harvest soon. The other room is ready for the light change to fruit. As we planned, we will be harvesting every two weeks and delivering two large crops at the end of every month."

"The holiday is over then," William said.

"Yes, for now, anyway."

They were very experienced: harvesting for two days, drying for a week and then bagging ready for delivery. This done, they moved on to taking cuttings from the mother plants and rooting them. They needed at least three hundred every two weeks to put under lights to join the beginning of their conveyor belt system. From then on, it was just a matter of checking the fertilizer levels and light timers. It meant a week's work altogether a month, including trimming off unnecessary leaves, and then it was ready for delivery. William made the call to arrange the meeting point and time; then, he hired a van.

"Right, Arthur, you go first on the motorbike; I will be five minutes behind with the van. If you see any sign of trouble or the police, phone or ride back to warn me. I will have my phone on all the time; best to be safe. Also, do a circuit of the meeting point to check them out, okay?"

"Suits me; let's go."

"Five minutes start then."

Arthur rode off, and William sat poised in the van. Five minutes duly passed, and William was soon up to the allotted speed of fifty mph. He cruised all the way without a problem. He pulled up alongside the buyer's vehicle and opened his door.

"Have you got the money?" William asked.

"Yes, here it is."

They swapped holdalls, each checking the contents.

William spoke first. "All looks good, as expected. We need to build up trust, so we would not expect anything silly. And, by the way, I put an extra one hundred-gram bag in for goodwill."

"Thanks. We will look forward to seeing you next month."

They drove off in opposite directions. It wasn't long before William saw Arthur behind on the motorbike. They pulled up for a quick chat.

"Anything to report, Arthur?"

"No. All okay. No one parked anywhere near."

"Let's go north to the motorway before heading home. We can have a baguette and coffee at the services and, of course, watch the traffic for a little while before heading home."

"See you there, then."

All these precautions had become second nature, but they preferred it that way.

"Well, that's another job done, William," Arthur said at the services.

"Yes, but it has made me think. I cannot see this one set-up and delivery being enough for our state of mind. I think it's going to be boring."

"I was thinking the same. Tomorrow, let's sit down and work out a plan to develop."

"Right, let us get to town, take the van back and have a beer. Then, you can carefully take me back home on the bike," William said and laughed.

The beer was welcome, and there were several fresh female faces, including quite a few holidaymakers and several new waitresses providing for them. William was soon busy chatting to the waitress of his choice, and Arthur had made his excuses and gone to another bar where he had spotted some possible entertainment. William's waitress was eager to talk.

"I have seen you and your friend a few times, but as you were always together, I thought you were a couple."

"Oh, no, definitely not! We have been best pals for years, but we are both more interested in female company. In fact, quite desperate, but we wanted to see how the land lies first. We did not want to tread on any toes or cause problems. Are you single?"

"Yes, very. I got out of a hopeless relationship a few months ago and came here to work and have a fresh start."

"Well, what's your name? I am William, and I would love to press your starter button."

"Well, I am Jane. I am a bit rusty, but for you, I will try to start first time."

"Wow! What time do you finish?"

"Well, it's summer and our busy season, so we stay open until 12.00."

"We have been out for a spin on the motor-bike, so we will take it back and be back here by 10 or so with the car. I will just go over and check that with Arthur."

William crossed the square and found Arthur in deep conversation with a very amused giggling lady. "Arthur, are you okay?"

With a wink, Arthur said, "Very, and you?"

"Yes, similar."

They both understood the code-like conversation.

"Arthur, I will take the bike back and get the car," William said. "Keep in touch by phone. Stay the night if you like. I probably will, you know, playing cards!!!"

"Okay, later, William. Bye, for now; good luck."

"And you, pal. Don't do anything I wouldn't do!"

"No, the same, only better," Arthur replied, laughing.

William rode home. The garage was locked up and tidy. He entered the house and unlocked the grow rooms, quickly checking the nutrients and that the light timers were working. Everything was good. Half an hour later, he had locked up again and was driving back to town, excited at the thought of what might happen. He had been without female company since escaping to France and missed it; he had his fingers crossed!

He parked and walked to the square; the whole place looked a hundred times more inviting. Across the tables of the restaurant, the waitress was smiling broadly at him. William looked the other way, across the square, at Arthur, who had his lady very close by now; they looked attached. Her head was resting on his shoulder, and she was still giggling. He gave a little wave, and Arthur, with a thumbs up to William, signalled it would be all night there, and then they would have breakfast together in town in the morning. They were as pleased for one another as much as pleased for themselves.

"Jane, do you live in town?" William asked.

"Yes, the restaurant has provided rooms for its staff, and yes, to answer your next question, you can stay. Please do. I have thought of little else since talking to you earlier."

"Me too, Jane, and Jane, I promise I am a gentleman."

"Don't worry, William. I can tell."

Midnight came. Arthur had disappeared, and Jane wanted nothing but to get back to her room and bed. As they undressed, there was no shyness on either side, and Jane certainly had nothing to be shy about. To William, she could not have looked more perfect; she was his ideal.

"You are beautiful dressed and even more so undressed, Jane. I am totally gobsmacked."

"You must have just got out of prison, William, to see me as special," she replied.

"Pardon my French, Jane, but, my dear, you are fucking special. And no, never in prison and don't ever intend to be. Come to me. I need to touch you to make sure you are real."

She came close and caressed him.

He touched her face, arms, legs, back, buttocks, perfect breasts and vagina saying, "I need to check every inch of you."

"Oh, yes, and me the same."

"It's an excuse for lots of foreplay. I can never get enough foreplay."

"Again, me too, William. My ex gave me none; he was useless."

They made love slowly. He made sure she had her orgasms before entertaining his own. Everything was perfect for him. When he needed to go for it himself aggressively, right on cue, she started shouting.

"Fuck me harder ... harder!"

And he did, as hard as possible. He could hold back no longer; he started to cum.

"William, William! God almighty, I am cumming again," she said, and with that, they collapsed and slept until morning.

Chapter 7

When they woke, light was streaming in. "What time do you have to work, Jane?"

"Ten o'clock, William," she said.

"Ah, that's good," he replied.

"We don't have to rush then."

"No, plenty of time. So, a cuddle first, then let's go for breakfast at the cafe on the corner in the sun," William suggested.

"That sounds good. But, William, I will need half an hour to wash and clean that well-fucked look off me before facing the world. If they guess, then they guess, but I would rather it did not look too obvious."

She seemed really happy, and he certainly was. As she dressed, he left a message for Arthur, asking if all was well. William informed him where they were going for breakfast and said to join them if convenient; otherwise, to let him know when and where to pick him up.

A message came back. "Hi, William. All good with me. I do not quite know where I am, but she will drive me to the cafe. I hope in time for breakfast with you two, but whatever, I will be there before ten to go home with you. See you soon."

As William and Jane walked to the cafe, she held his arm. He had had casual affairs before and felt guilty, especially if the lady concerned showed affection in public, but not this time! This time, he was proud to feel her hand; in fact, he would have been very disappointed if she had not held him. They reached the cafe, and he pulled a chair out for her. Their eyes met; they both smiled.

He knew what her eyes were saying, and his look left her in no doubt as to how he was feeling, especially as he said for anyone close to hear, "Jane, you really are gorgeous."

They were sitting eating breakfast, enjoying each other's company when another happy couple arrived.

"Good morning, William. This is my very good friend, Angelina," Arthur announced.

"Well, good morning to you both. Please join us for breakfast. This is ... er, er, what's your name?" he half-joked as his mind went blank.

Jane slapped him on the shoulder, and he quickly remembered.

"Jane, Jane! How could I forget?"

"That's better. But what is your name?" joked Jane.

"Jane, excuse my friend, William; he just must joke," Arthur interjected.

"Do you and William live together?" she asked.

"Yes. Separate rooms, of course," he said. "William came along over ten years ago and literally saved me from a desperate depression. He provided me with the will to survive and a whole new life. We have been like brothers ever since."

William added, "We went our own ways for a time, when all of a sudden, I found myself in a very serious life-threatening situation. Arthur here arrived in the nick of time; he put himself in danger but saved me. By the time we had sorted out all the problems, we both accepted destiny had shown us twice that we were meant to stay close. So here we are – a new beginning in the south of France. We think alike, we never argue, and as you can see, we both need the company of attractive women."

"I second that," Arthur said.

"Now, ask no more questions, and let us enjoy breakfast," William said.

"William and me are going to be busy for a few days, but how about a trip to Andorra for the four of us? A day out and a bit of shopping?" Pointing at William, Arthur added, "He definitely needs new socks and underwear, and a few bottles of wine and whiskey would be good."

"So there you are, girls. Arrange a day off and consider yourselves dated or pulled, okay?" William said.

"I like the idea. How about you, Angelina?" Jane asked.

"Oh, yes, me too. Let's exchange numbers. As soon as we arrange a day, we will let you Brothers Grimm know and leave you to arrange everything."

They all laughed. There was a four-way bond forming; they were all appreciating this social life.

A quick kiss on both cheeks and they parted; Jane for work, and Angelina to her friends at the holiday cottage they had rented.

The boys drove home to find Tom working away happily. "All okay, Tom?" Arthur asked.

"Yes, no problems. The postman came – that's all."

"Tom, can you find time in the next couple of days to service and check over the BMW? We are planning a trip up the mountains at the end of the week."

"Sure, Arthur, with pleasure. When you don't need it, leave it by the garage door, and I will see to it."

"Thanks, Tom."

They unlocked and went in. Soon they were working in the grow rooms, potting up the baby plants, taking another three hundred cuttings and transferring a further four hundred to the fruiting room: their final destination until ready for harvesting. They both enjoyed the work and said very little; they were amazingly alike in word and deed. Two hours later, they had finished and were sat with yet another coffee in the garden.

"This is the life, Arthur. I took it for granted you were happy with Angelina. I certainly am with Jane."

"Oh, yes, Angelina was great. Perfect for now; then, later, we'll see. Perhaps more. Let's not think too far ahead. Anything could happen. *Carpe diem*, William."

"Yes! Oh, by the way, I put the holdall in the grow room locker. Could you divide it up? We need to stash it away as usual. While you do that, I will pay the bills here. Tomorrow, I am going to town for lunch at the place where Jane works. I am thinking of having a load of firewood delivered here, ready for winter. We might not need it, but anyone watching won't need to know how we are keeping warm. I spoke to Tom earlier. He has a pal who will cut our lawns and hedges once a week for a price; it is starting to look untidy. Oh, and Arthur, how about phoning Angelina to see if she is free for you to collect her on the motorbike and take her for a spin later? I bet she would love it, and I know you will!!!!"

"Are you sure, William? I don't want to leave you with all the work."

"Arthur, I am not busy, and I really like the idea of you thrilling Angelina. Enjoy, Arthur. Go for it."

"I will. Great! See you tonight."

"I hope so," William laughed.

Very soon, a grinning Arthur rode off with a spare helmet ready on the back.

William went to town and had lunch served by a happy Jane. "Arthur has gone on the motorbike to take Angelina for a ride. I hope she is not the nervous type because he is a great rider. She will have the thrill of her life."

"William, can we do that sometime?"

"Of course we can. Anytime you like, but you might want to bring spare pants with you," he warned, laughing.

"Don't worry, William. I love a thrill and trust you implicitly."

"Okay, Jane, we will do that soon, but first, have you arranged your day off and spoken to Angelina ?"

"Yes, Monday morning early, and make a day of it. She will be here at 8 am for breakfast, and then we all go. Is that okay with you two?"

"Yes, we will come for breakfast at 8 am as well, and I can speak for both of us; we are looking forward to it. We have some work to do, and it's the weekend already, so if not before, we will be here at 8 on Monday. I need to get back now; I am having wood delivered this afternoon."

"Bye then, William."

"Bye, for now, sweetheart! See you Monday."

He got back home as the wood arrived and had it tipped close to the shed at the back door.

He soon stacked it inside the dry building. It was supposed to have been cut for at least two years to make it dry and ready to burn hot. It still looked a bit green, but they would manage. Perhaps they would need to split it further before burning it.

Next, he went in to check the grow rooms. Everything was running like clockwork. He topped up the nutrients and stripped off all the bottom leaves from the bigger plants. He was happy in his work and probably stayed working longer than necessary. He was thinking about Jane all the time, which made it pass quickly. Not long after he finished and sat with a beer downstairs, he heard the motorbike arrive, its lights winging around the yard outside.

"Thanks for suggesting that, William; she loved it," Arthur said. "By the time we stopped at a quiet private spot, she was so turned on. I said nothing; she literally tore her pants off, saying, 'I need you now, Arthur, for fuck's sake, now.' I put the bike on its stand, dropped my jeans and sat on the tank facing back. She sat facing me, her legs around me, feet sometimes on the handlebars, sometimes around my neck. She was ferocious, desperate to get it all in her. Once in, there was no escape and no way out. She hit, bit, scratched and swore foully at me. I thought it would never end. I could not tell one of her orgasms from the next – perhaps it was one that lasted an hour. I have no idea. But I certainly have no complaints: long live randy women!

"No sooner had she finished, she got off and stood there, semen running down her legs, saying, 'Sorry, Arthur, sorry!!' At the same time, I was saying, 'Thank you, thank you, Angelina. Do not be sorry; that was spectacular. I only have one worry.' 'What's that, Arthur?' she said, and I said, 'Well, sexy bitch, it is going to be embarrassing if you react the same when we stop at your house!!' We both laughed a lot, and she said, 'I promise I will hide it and act as normal as possible for any onlookers.' She just about managed it, apart from squeezing my hand when saying goodnight."

"Well, Arthur. Who is a lucky boy, then?? I am jealous. Next week I am taking Jane for a ride; I'll keep my fingers crossed for something similar!! By the way, the grass has been cut, and the firewood is in the shed. I checked the plants – all okay, and we are booked for Monday and Andorra. Breakfast in town with the girls, then away."

"Wonderful, William. What would I do without you? I have to go to bed now; I am knackered. Talk in the morning."

"Goodnight, Arthur. Glad you are back safe."

"Goodnight, pal. Thanks for being you."

"Ditto, Arthur, ditto."

Chapter 8

The morning brought a brand new day.

"Bring your coffee out and look at the garden, Arthur," William said. "He has cut the grass and pruned most of the fruit trees. He is coming back today to cut the hedges. I have shown him where to have his bonfire for all his trimmings. He wants 50 euros this time, but most weeks, only 20 as it will only be the grass. What do you think?"

"Seems fair. Certainly looks a lot better."

"We need an hour or so tonight checking the plants as it is Monday tomorrow, and we will be away all day. Tom has serviced the car, so we are ready.

"Let's have a lazy day today," Arthur suggested.

"Suits me, and we can spend time thinking about what to do with the business from now on."

"I have been thinking about that. First decision: do we want a series of small growers to buy from? Then next: where do we want to sell it?"

"Well, first, if we buy from other growers, they will need to be at least sixty kilometres apart. Secondly, we do not want to deliver far, as the further we deliver, the more danger there is," William warned.

"Okay, whenever we are out, we keep our ears open for contacts. If we find the right people, it might be worth us supplying the equipment; then they would owe us loyalty!" Arthur said.

"The one golden rule, as usual, must be never to expose to anyone who we are or where we are from."

"Well, William, that's sorted then."

"Even on Monday in Andorra, keep a lookout. Let's face it, Andorra and the mountains are full of fun-loving trippers skiing and willing to pay top dollar for good stuff. The main thing is we need good contacts, and for this project, we are Bill and Ben."

"Well, William, you had better be Ben, as William and Bill are too similar."

"Okay, Bill, we are ready then."

They were up early on Monday morning, meticulously securing the rooms and house. By 8 am, they were in the cafe with coffee, waiting for the ladies before ordering breakfast; they had not arrived yet.

"I suppose it's a woman's prerogative to be late," Arthur said.

"Yes, that's okay. We have plenty of time."

They soon arrived, and the four ordered. They ate and enjoyed the early morning meeting.

"Do you want to drive, Arthur?" William asked.

"I would like that."

Jane spoke up. "You men take the front. Angelina and me have lots to talk about that would not interest either of you, so we will be happy in the back."

"Right, let's go."

They drove halfway, then started the steady climb up the Pyrenees and soon stopped to admire the view. All were very impressed. They drove on, seeing more and more snow on the roadside. They parked near the shops and went for a look around. As a joke, Jane made William buy socks and underwear, as Arthur had suggested. Most things were cheap; some very cheap. They all bought things, and the boys treated the girls. They locked everything in the car and went for lunch.

They found a restaurant with good views of the ski slopes. They sat comfortably watching, and lunch took some time, but still, they were reluctant to leave. However, the time had come, and they needed to shop for cheap booze and tobacco.

They bought well over the legal limit to cross back into France, but as William said, "Fingers crossed and look innocent. It's worth the chance anyway. The worst thing that could happen would be that we have to pay the tax, so let us live dangerously, ha ha ha."

As they got to the border, the police called the *Douane* looked officious but just waved them through. Further on, they stopped again for the view, and William opened the boot.

"You got the Golden Virginia then, Arthur?"

"Yes, and the man from the shop packed it in as tight as possible."

Both girls stood open-mouthed, looking at all this tobacco.

"I did not tell you girls about this in case you looked guilty at the crossing."

"You are right; I would have been crapping myself if I had known," Jane admitted.

"Me too," Angelina said. "So if our faces had not given the game away, then the smell definitely would have."

"What on earth are you going to do with all that?" Jane asked.

"We have a buyer willing to pay us over double," William replied, "and they're still buying it at half the normal price. We paid three thousand euros for it, we sell it for six thousand, and it is worth over nine. So, everyone wins. This is first-class rolling tobacco in big demand everywhere. Just one problem. We need to unload it at our yard before going into town."

They stopped.

"So this is where you two live," Jane said.

"Yes, this is home," William said. "We have not finished renovating the house yet. You can come and see some of it while we unload. Arthur, take the girls in while I unload. It won't take long; then we can go to town."

"Well, one thing's for sure," Jane observed, "there's no woman living here."

Angelina added, "No, but it will be nice when it is finished. The garden is looking nice."

William came in to join them. "All is stored away. Shall we go to town?"

"We are ready."

They parked as usual by the church and strolled to a bar. It had been a tiring day for all four of them.

"I hope you girls enjoyed your day. We did, didn't we, Arthur? Four beers, is it? Or something else?"

They both answered, "Beer is good."

Although there was not much chat, they all felt content like two married couples.

William and Arthur had a quiet talk. Both agreed to stay the night with their ladies and meet in the morning for breakfast at eight, as usual, then go back to work. They had to harvest that day and dry, ready to deliver at the end of the week. They needed to get stuck in and work on their new project, searching different areas for buyers to buy from.

"Time for my bed, Arthur. You take the car and Angelina and see me in the morning."

"Sure, William, I won't be late. Can we go, Angelina? I do not know about you, but I am tired."

"I am ready. Let's go. Goodnight, you two. Thanks for a lovely day."

"Let's go, Jane," William said. "I need my beauty sleep. You don't!"

"Okay, ugly, let's go."

The foursome split up, only to meet again in the morning for breakfast.

After breakfast, the boys headed off home to work. Once again, as they drove in, a busy Tom waved a thumbs up to let them know all was okay. They unlocked, went in, and got straight on with the harvesting of the fruiting room. It took all day, but at the end of it, there was a large crop hanging in the drying room. In five or six days, when it was dry enough, it would get its final trim and then be weighed and vacuum-packed in one hundred-gram packs, ready for delivery. William had rung the buyer to offer him the chance to buy some of the tobacco. Everyone who buys cannabis needs tobacco, so of course, the buyer readily agreed to buy half of it, knowing it would sell and give him another easy profit.

All the rooms were altered again. The recently emptied rooms were filled again, and more cuttings were taken to grow on for a future harvest where it would go into a grow room as soon as one became available. All went like clockwork, as usual.

They drove into the mountains, hoping to find contacts and possible growers. It did not take them long; several hippy communes were only too willing to up their production for a regular sale. In less than a week, they had got four new growers happy to supply. It would not be the same strength or quality as the boys, but it was good enough and sellable. But the boys grew under perfect conditions. They had agreed on a sensible price and would collect once a month.

William made the call and arranged the delivery point. He loaded the van along with the tobacco and drove off again, five minutes behind his diligent pal Arthur. It did feel a lot safer having a different delivery point each time, driving home in a different direction, taking the long way round and stopping to double-check for followers. This time, the haversack was transferred to Arthur on the motorbike. He took it home, collected the car and then went to the van hire office for William. Both were then ready for town and a beer with, of course, the friendly faces of the ladies.

Jane's first words were, "Stay tonight, William, please. I missed you!"

"With pleasure, sweetheart. But let me talk with Arthur. I think it will suit him too."

"Arthur, are you staying tonight? I am."

"Yes, I have just arranged it."

"Good. Two happy boys and two happy girls, I think. Breakfast here in the morning, as usual, then. I will just have a quick word with Jane; she has to work for another couple of hours. I'll come back and have a drink with you two."

He was soon back and out of her way as she worked. "Well, Angelina," William said, "Arthur and me have had a hard few days, but we are free for a while again. We need to contact associates in the UK. We are buying some machines to bring over to hire out, so soon, it will be all go again. We do seem to be finding our way here, don't we, Arthur? You are happy in France, especially with this lovely lady! I will wander over to Jane; she will finish soon. See you both for breakfast."

Chapter 9

It was much more of a loving night for both couples, more personal than frantic sex, all four smiling happily at breakfast.

Angelina had a request. "Can all four of us have a day out later this week as my holiday is nearly over, and my friends and I will have to go back to Paris the week after?"

"Oh dear, I had not thought of that," Arthur said. "Of course we can, and perhaps we can arrange visits to Paris and for you to come back here."

"It is certainly not goodbye. Well, not from me, anyway. Let's not talk about that now; we will arrange something. When is your next day off, Jane?"

"Wednesday, if it suits you two. Unless Arthur and you, Angelina, would prefer to go somewhere alone?" Jane replied.

So, Arthur, sort it out with Angelina, and we will go along with whatever you decide. Car or motorbike, hotel on the Mediterranean or up the mountain. I can manage on my own anyway. Today, it's back to work for us. Bye, girls, talk later."

They drove off. William's first job would be to check the plants and watering system. Arthur was to divide the cash and stash it away again safely. These tasks were done by midday, so they sat in their cut and trimmed garden for lunch.

"It can be heaven here, William, don't you think?"

"Yes, and it will stay like it as long as we keep developing and conquer the boredom with a bit of danger or, of course, the excitement of a good woman. What do you think she will choose to do when you ring her later?"

"I have a feeling she will choose a couple of days on the motorbike somewhere, probably up the mountain. It's an adrenalin thing: she loves the buzz."

"Well, whatever. Good luck to you both. Just be careful, pal."

"Yes, of course."

"And I will probably spend the nights you are away keeping Jane happy in town."

"The machines should arrive next week. I just hope they have found and removed all the trackers. I bought them from Paris in the name of Andrews brothers. I have arranged for them to be collected from Paris and delivered to Toulouse, where the local boys will collect them for us after they have been painted in our business colours – Andrews brothers blue."

"Go and ring Angelina, Arthur."

"I will now."

He was soon back. "I was right. It's me on the motorbike up over the Pyrenees for two days. Are you sure that is alright with you?"

"Of course it is. I am pleased for you!"

Wednesday soon came, and off went Arthur; they came back Friday night.

"Sorry, William. We were having such a good time; we did not want it to end."

"That is okay. It all went easily; I never missed you," he said, laughing. "The machines are ready and painted in Toulouse, waiting for collection. Next week is harvest week again. After that, we collect from the hippies and then deliver at the end of that week, so a couple of busy weeks. And I think we need another Tom who can drive machines and run that business. It's probably a good idea to ask Tom if he knows anyone; I bet he does."

And he did. The machines arrived, and so did Tom's pal, Julian, who was only too pleased to have a job with regular pay. This yard was becoming a real hub of industry.

"Julian, we would like to give you a trial run. The business will be in your name. We will split the profits after costs, calling our half rent for the yard and machines. A diesel tank is coming for industrial diesel. It will be easy enough to work out at the end of every month. Do you want to give it a try renting them out with or without you as a driver? We will pay you a retainer for the first month to get you started, and of course, any money you charge for driving, you keep. What do you think?"

"I think I would be a fool if I did not accept your offer, so thank you very much. When do I start? I never had the money to buy machines, or I would already be doing it."

"Okay, then. Start as soon as you like. Your first job will be to scrape the yard and make room for the diesel tank by the side over there. We have a couple of builders interested in hiring. They will both be here on Monday to talk to you. One thing, please keep everything straight, as Arthur never misses anything. And, Julian, I am sure Tom will tell you, be good to us, and we will be good to you."

"Tom already has recommended you highly. I will be here at 8 am tomorrow."

"The keys are on the hook in that shed office. Good luck and welcome, Julian."

William went in to talk to Arthur. "All arranged, Arthur. Now for us, harvest tomorrow, and the day after, we collect from the hippies. Fingers crossed that they have done a good job. The next day will be new cuttings day, end of the week, we pack up all the dried bud, ready for delivery. I have spoken to the buyer and offered him a fair deal for any extra stuff; he is pleased. I can see to everything. See as much as you can of Angelina before she goes."

"Okay, William. Thanks."

William collected from the hippies, paid them and left them with a message. "If it is good stuff, I will be back at the end of the month to buy all you want to sell. If it is poor, then think yourselves lucky. Keep the money but no more business, understood?"

"Yes, fully, thank you, but we are sure you will like it."

He drove off. As soon as he was back, he could see Arthur was ready to go to town.

"Arthur, you go. I have things to do here, so see you tomorrow, okay?"

"Yes, I will be back first thing."

"No hurry, enjoy."

William sat upstairs watching over the yard; Julian had levelled and cleared it. He had parked the machines neatly where they could be seen from the road and where passers-by could read the hire signs written on them. He watched Julian lock them up. By then, Tom had locked the garage and spoken to Julian before they both left for their homes. Satisfied with outside, William turned his attention to the plants and nutrients. This all done, he went downstairs for a sandwich before having an early night.

He was up early as usual in the morning, trimming and packing the latest dried crop. He had done it all, loaded the van, and even checked the new plants before 8 am. From his vantage point upstairs, he saw Tom and Julian arrive. They unlocked, and Tom went to the machines, checking the oil and water before starting his own work at the garage. William liked what he saw and went down for breakfast and coffee. He was happily waiting for Arthur. There was plenty of time, and he still had to phone the buyer to arrange today's meeting point.

Arthur came in. "Ready when you are."

"No hurry. Have coffee and sit for a while. I will make the arrangements. Let's leave in an hour, Arthur."

The arrangements were made, and Arthur was calm with his head in a better place. He left on the hour with William the usual five minutes behind. Arthur reached the point and made a wide circle out of the buyer's vision. He spotted a car watching from a nearby lane. He stopped and phoned William, who also stopped.

"William, binoculars, 150 metres behind: two occupants."

"Thanks, I will rearrange. You stay watching the watchers." William rang the buyer. "Do you want to do this deal, fool? If so, tell your backup not to move until we have met somewhere else. They are in our sights!! Do you understand?"

"Yes, my mistake."

"How much of a mistake, dumbo?"

"I promise not a big one; nothing serious."

"This is a serious business; we are not beginners. Now we'll meet on our own at a new site. Travel west on the D8 until I tell you to turn off. First, tell your watchers not to move for half an hour, or they will suffer."

"I will phone them now," the buyer said, hanging up the phone.

William called Arthur. "Arthur, I have put half an hour's stop on the binoculars. Watch them then meet me on the motorway services where we met last time. I have sorted it; thanks, Arthur. I always know I can rely on you."

"Well done, William. See you later."

William called the buyer back. "Now, fool, when you reach the crossroads, turn left and drive to the first rough layby on the right. I will get there soon. Be ready to pay. I won't be staying there longer than necessary."

"Okay, I am at the crossroads, so I will be there in minutes."

"And I am behind you now," William said.

They pulled in together.

William checked the cash closely, having lost the original trust.

"We were just being careful," the buyer explained.

"This is a business that has to be built on trust. That was your one and only mistake. The next problem of any sort there will be big and fast punishment."

"Sorry, a stupid mistake. It won't happen again."

William spoke sharply. "You have had your warning." He then drove off, changing direction a couple of times, but still arrived at the services before Arthur.

"All okay, William?"

"Yes, thanks to you."

"The watchers never left the car; they just sat riveted in their seats. They looked shocked. They just did not know where they were being watched from. In the end, I rode away quietly. I think it will be okay now, but we will continue our vigilance."

"Same as last time. You take the haversack back home and stash it away. I will take the van back, so pick me up from the town with the car in an hour or so. Oh, and casually check on Tom and Julian; then we won't have to hurry home."

"Okay, William. I will just poke my head into the grow rooms to check on that while I am there. See you later." He took the haversack and rode off.

William headed for town to hand in the van before walking to see Jane, who was busy at work.

"Hi, gorgeous. Arthur will be here soon, and we would like lunch served by my favourite waitress."

It was not long before Arthur was there, eating lunch as well.

"When is Angelina's last day, Arthur?" William asked.

"They leave later today."

"Drop me off after lunch and go say your goodbyes. She will appreciate it."

As they drove home, they discussed the day.

"What happens now, William? Do you trust them?" Arthur asked.

"I think so, but we should find another buyer for at least half of it. I have the idea that as the deal was getting bigger and nearer to their limit, it was making us a target!! Less to sell means less of a target. What do you think?"

"You are the man, William. A perfect assessment, I think. They are not a big operation, but the amount involved was giving them ideas above their station."

"We are both right, Arthur; only you put it better. Great minds think alike," he said, laughing.

As they drove in, Tom was working away on one machine, and Julian was obviously out.

"All okay, Tom?" William asked through the open car window.

"Yes, no problems. Julian has taken the maxi lift to the big site. They have booked him for a couple of weeks, so he is happy. Otherwise, no callers."

They parked the car.

"I will reorganise the grow rooms, then chill out," William said. "You go to Angelina and help her pack," he added, chuckling.

"Yes, William, and if it's okay with you, I will take the motorbike. It gives her memories and is easier to use."

"Right. See you sometime tonight. Tomorrow we will find another buyer – up in the ski areas, perhaps."

"Sure, that would be an asset up there. Plan our route while I am out, Mr Organiser."

"Right, Mr Minder."

William worked away in the grow rooms, moving pots and plants to their next stages, stripping leaves and topping up water and nutrients. Satisfied there, he went to the kitchen for coffee. He sat with his map when he remembered a conversation he had had in Andorra with the owner of a tobacco shop after buying from him on his last visit. The shop owner had offered to deliver anything over the border into France as he knew several off-road routes that he used to avoid problems. Well, Mr Organiser thought that is where they would start: that man was bound to know a buyer. In the morning, the boys would head straight over the border to Andorra and that man's shop. It was far from the biggest shop, but that meant he would be more understanding and approachable.

Chapter 10

By 9 am, they were ready to go. All checked and locked, they went for a quick chat with Tom; he was as punctual as ever.

"How is it going, Tom?" Arthur asked.

"Another busy day for me and Julian. He has gone straight to the site. He has his phone, and I will keep an eye open for anyone needing to see him. Are you two off out?"

"Yes, business in Andorra," William replied, "so probably not back until late afternoon. Do you need anything while we are out?"

"No, but could you get me a carton of cigarettes while you are up there?"

"Of course, no problem, we will do that. But try to give it up. You will feel so much better, or at least cut down."

"I will try. I know you are right."

"Okay, see you later."

They drove without rushing and parked in Andorra before lunch. They sat with dinner watching the skiing. That done, it was time to visit Adrian at his shop.

"Good morning, Adrian," William said as they entered. "How are you today?"

"Pretty quiet at the moment, but then it is in the afternoons when it gets busy – and evenings, of course."

"Well, we won't beat around the bush. We have a question and probably a proposition for you. After talking to you last time, we both thought you were the right man: one that we could safely approach. Adrian, we collect from several growers but prefer to deliver and sell in one go to a secure source. The question is, do you know anyone suitable, or could you handle it yourself?"

"Well, boys, that was direct. I do appreciate your honesty, and I am up for extra business. Now, I do have people here to pass anything on to in one lump: good, trustworthy people. And I can add something on to this. As I mentioned before, I do know several routes over the mountains without ever being close to the border checkpoints. For a fee, I can collect in France and deliver to my sources here. That way, neither they nor you will need to worry about exposure. Let me show you this map. If you see here, just south of the border, is a plateau – a perfect meeting point. For a sensible price, I would like to buy from you there, and then you no longer have a problem. How about that?"

"That is exactly what we hoped for, and we can definitely give you a good reduction in price. The happier we all are, the better. Adrian, you are not French; you are from Andorra, yes?"

"Oh, yes, why?"

"We, as Englishmen, like to shake hands. An Englishman's handshake is his unbreakable bond. A Frenchman's is worthless. I hope a man from Andorra has the same value as an Englishman."

"Mine is the same as yours, boys. Trust is the most valuable thing. I want to shake hands with you both."

They shook and became three happy gentlemen!

"Right, that done, we would like to buy some cartons of cigarettes and some bottles of alcohol from you," William said. "Then, the next thing you will hear from us will be a WhatsApp message with a date to meet, but no time as the time will always be twelve midday. Is that suitable for you?"

"Great, William. As professional as ever."

They bought Tom's cigarettes and their evening tipples and headed for home.

"Job well done, William."

"Well done again, Arthur."

They drove straight back home. Neither felt much like socialising, just a quiet night, a few drinks in their garden with pleasant music that suited them both. Lately, they had been living on the edge. They pulled up at the garage and handed Tom his cigarettes.

"Here, Tom. Present for you," Arthur said.

"Wow, thanks, fellas. Are you sure?"

"Yes, enjoy, but try to stop. We need you."

"I will try."

They did check their plants, but it had become second nature and was quickly done. Music on, glasses in hand, they sat quietly relaxing in the garden. Perhaps this was the calm before the storm. William, for one, was thinking things had gone so well for so long it was beginning to feel inevitable that something would go wrong – it probably had to soon!

"Arthur, would you like to go to Paris for a few days? I can manage easily here at the moment, so now is a good time, but in ten days, we will be busy again."

"Yes, if that is alright with you, William. I will go tomorrow."

"Take the BMW. I have the van and the bike, and I fancy using the bike; the weather is perfect for it."

"William, I need a break. I will pack tonight and call her and leave in the morning, all being well." There was a lift in Arthur's demeanour. He rang Angelina, who was pleased with the news.

He was soon packed. Both men had become used to travelling light. "By the way, William, I have got the list of number plates of everyone we know and/or deal with, plus any suspicious ones. I will make you a copy. Do not leave home without one. I will also have one. You never know! Watch everything."

"Yes, I know you are right. To be careful is to be safe."

In the morning, Arthur left, and William spent an hour talking to Tom. He gave him the list of number plates to watch out for and asked him to write down any others that seemed to be hanging around.

"Arthur is visiting his lady friend for a week, so I will probably be around here a lot more," William explained. "Also, I have a lot of paperwork to catch up on, and him being away gives me a good chance to do it all quickly, uninterrupted."

There was not really much paperwork, but he needed the excuse to be in a lot without interruption. Harvesting the latest crop on his own and hanging it to dry while Arthur was away would save a lot of time when he came back, and they would be ready to deliver again. He also needed to construct a system for disposing of the old, stripped plants and overused soil from the pots without it being recognised. He bought a high-sided tipping trailer that could be parked underneath a rear window once a fortnight. All the unwanted rubbish could be dropped in, taken to the bonfire, tipped, burnt and then covered, with nothing left to be seen. 'Arthur will be pleased with that,' he thought. He soon finished his so-called paperwork. The crop was drying well and would be ready to pack when Arthur came back.

That afternoon, he locked up, spoke to Tom and drove to town for a long-needed treat and meeting with the neglected Jane. "Sorry, Jane,

I have been very busy, and Arthur is away. I have missed you a lot, so if you can forgive me, I am here now and would like to arrange a day out for the two of us as soon as possible."

"Well, I have been pretty fed up, but you are here now, so I suppose you are forgiven. Tomorrow is my day off. What do you suggest?"

"I suggest I stay tonight, and in the morning, we head out on the motorbike. Arthur has got the car, and the weather is still good."

"I will enjoy the motorbike. Are you hungry, William?"

"A bit. Wait on me, Jane. I will pay the bill now, but you will get your tip later."

"It had better be more than the tip, meanie."

"We will have to see," he joked. The food was good, the evening better, the night tremendous, and the company perfect.

The breakfast in the morning was a great start to the day. "Where shall we go?" William asked.

"Anywhere you want," Jane replied.

"Well, I need to find a village on the plateau. We will do that first, then over the border to Andorra as it is close. A bit of shopping, then back down the mountain. Any time will do for me, as I can stay the night again tonight if you like."

"You know I would like that."

"Let's go then."

The plateau and the village were easy to find, and the journey through the wild countryside was lovely. "Let us have coffee here," Jane suggested, "then lunch in Andorra. How far is it?"

"Less than half an hour, but the main road way takes half an hour; we will still be early when we get there."

"It is a lovely spot here. By the way, what is that list of numbers stuck on the bike tank?"

"That, my love, is a list of number plates I need to watch out for – problem ones."

"William, am I in danger? Have you upset someone? You two do seem to be very secretive."

"We are in no danger, but both me and Arthur like to be one jump ahead; there are always jealous businessmen around. Anyway, no one knows this bike, and I like to see where people come from for future reference."

They rode to the mountain road, up through the border crossing and into Andorra. At least with the motorbike, it was easy to park, so they rode to their favourite restaurant and parked right outside. They were both ready for lunch and spent a comfortable hour there before venturing along the mountaintop roads. They enjoyed the panoramic views while finding the perfect hotel for the night.

"Let us stay here the night, Jane. If we make a reasonable start in the morning, I can get you back in plenty of time for work."

"That would be wonderful. I don't start until eleven tomorrow, so we've plenty of time."

"Let's book in. I fancy a beer on that veranda to watch the sun go down. How about you?"

"We have no luggage; will it be alright?" Jane asked.

"I will see to it," William said.

He arranged a good room with a view. The hotel was not busy, and they were probably used to couples staying without much luggage. It was a lovely evening, but William was still having, as he had done for the past couple of weeks, a feeling of foreboding as, for a long while, everything had gone too good to be true. Was this the calm before the storm? This had been the longest calm he had ever experienced. He pushed these nags to one side. Perhaps if he was careful not to put the devil on the wall, his luck could last forever.

Chapter 11

They rode happily back, taking all different roads. At the bottom of the mountain, the roads levelled out. William slowed and stopped. "Wait here, Jane. I won't be a minute." He walked back to a vantage point overlooking a large house where he had spotted a car with a number plate he recognised in the drive; it was the watcher's car. He spent the next few minutes walking around the area, checking out every aspect of that house. At the moment, there was no real reason, but second nature had always been worth taking notice of, and you never know when it could be useful – this was the buyer's house!!

He walked back to Jane. "Sorry, Jane, but I spotted one of those number plates at a house back there and went back to check it."

"We are still early."

"Let's go then."

Within the hour, they were back in town.

"Thanks, William. That was a perfect break."

"Perfect for me, too, Jane. It is always great for me when you are around. Don't work too hard. See you soon. Arthur is back in a couple of days. I need to tidy up and sort business out, ready for him." He waved, and she blew him a kiss as he rode off.

He was soon in the yard. He pulled up by Tom and Julian; they were having their morning break. He got off the bike and found a box to sit with them.

"All good, boys?" William asked.

"Yes," they replied in unison.

He smiled and joked, "Arthur is due back, so I have a lot of housework to do. By the way, Tom, have any of those number plates been around at all yet?"

"No, and I tend to look at number plates all the time now – it has become second nature!"

William spent the morning in the grow rooms, checking water levels, stripping lower leaves and looking at plant welfare. Lastly, he felt the hanging harvest. It was drying well; another day, and it would be ready to weigh and pack for delivery. He phoned the hippies. It was good news; they would be ready for him to collect from later that week.

By the end of the day, all was up to date, ready for Arthur's return late the next afternoon. Now there was time to relax. He sat in the garden that had been cut and trimmed again. It improved after every cut; it was becoming quite idyllic. Unfortunately, this did not remove the nagging sense of foreboding. It was no longer just in the back of his mind but was becoming a permanent thought.

Nevertheless, Arthur arrived back safely, much to William's relief.

"All okay here, William?"

"Yes. How did you find Paris?"

"I had a great time but would not want to live there full time. I was ready to come home today. Sad to leave Angelina, but I am not cut out to holiday day after day; I need a purpose. Two or three days is enough."

"Well, settle in today. We have collections and deliveries to do tomorrow. Harvest is done; I needed the work to occupy my mind. Tomorrow, after breakfast, I want to collect from the hippies and deliver to Adrian on the plateau. I found the place while you were away. I will show you on the map."

They were up early and did not need breakfast, both eager to be off. "First, hire the van. I will follow you with the car today, William," Arthur said.

"Right, the weather is cooling rapidly."

William hired the van and was about to drive out when Arthur stopped him.

"William, do not look round. Act normal, but the watchers are watching us. Their car is parked between those two vans watching all we do. They are obviously expecting you to deliver to them with the van, as usual. What do you suggest?"

"Arthur, I think you should stay with the van. Drive it into town and have lunch. I am sure they will watch the van, hoping to know where we live or where we get the cannabis from. I will slip off to the hippies and the plateau to meet Adrian. Good luck. Keep in touch, and don't let them know you have seen them."

"Any problems or changes, I will phone you."

"Right, I will slip off."

The watchers continued to watch Arthur apparently busying himself around the van before driving into town for lunch. He intended to waste at least an hour there, every now and again messaging William to let him know all was going to plan.

William collected from the hippies and was soon at the plateau with Adrian. Neither wasted any time, and they parted within a few minutes. Second nature led William to take a long way around, going home and then to a meeting point with Arthur. He collected the stock from home and drove fifty-odd kilometres to the far side of town, where he met Arthur.

"Are they still watching, Arthur?"

"No, I lost them when I drove out of town."

"Well, I am loaded again in the car and have arranged to deliver again to Adrian. He is excited to get extra! While I do that, you waste time here before going back to town to hand the van back. I will r the car back and collect you on the motorbike at six o'clock. If they are still watching by then, we will soon lose them again, and if they have recognised the car, I will park it in the shed well out of sight."

"Well, I think that covers everything for now," Arthur said.

William delivered to Adrian again with no problem. He then drove, taking another route back home and parked the car out of sight in the back of the shed. He then rode the bike the long way to town. He collected Arthur and chose yet another route back home. Very soon, he lost the watchers. He hid the bike in the shed with the car. Once in the house, Arthur divided the money and stashed it away.

"Tomorrow, Arthur, we need to have a serious talk," William said. "We have been lucky so far because of our attention to detail. But things are getting more difficult every day now. It is time for a serious change. Everything is up to date here, so we have time to plan. First thing: we need to check with Tom and Julian to see if they have noticed anyone hanging around near here. Also, it might be time to change the car. I expect they clocked it today somewhere, and if they did not, they soon will. I am supposed to ring them to arrange a delivery in the next two or three days, and I expect a backlash as soon as they realise it is not going to happen! Do I tell them why or say nothing and leave them thinking we have not seen them following?"

"Say nothing. We could still find it useful."

"Yes, I think the same. While you were away, I found where they live, but I still think they do not know where we are based. The longer that lasts, the better, or we will have to shut down. Right, we have a decision to make today. We hire a van and act as though all is normal. Do we arrange and deliver them some to keep them a bit happy for now, or do we cut them off from now? You decide, Arthur."

"Well, I think, deliver some as usual with a message that we are not getting as much from our suppliers – in fact, we might have to finish. That should lead them away from thinking we are growing ourselves."

"Okay, let us give it a try. I will bag up some and make the call."

"And I will take it to the other side of the village with our old truck, park, and wait for you to arrive with the van load, as though we have collected from somewhere in that area. You drive the truck back to town and collect the motorbike. I will give you a fifteen-minute head start to check out the meeting point. I will then deliver and explain the drop in produce. We then take the long way round back, but we must be extra observant this time."

Arthur checked the site, and William delivered to a disappointed buyer, who seemed to believe the story. The boys headed home. They dropped the van off and headed for the truck.

"William, you take the bike and the money. I will take the truck on a long route just in case they are still watching. I will ring in an hour to arrange where to leave it, and you can collect me."

So far, so good. William was soon home undetected. Cash stashed away, he sat waiting for Arthur's call.

It was getting late, so he decided to go and find him. He rode to and straight through the town before searching the roads. He soon found the truck. It had careered off the road, down the bank and into a tree. There was a lot of blood in the truck but no Arthur. The inside of the vehicle had been wrenched apart and thoroughly searched. William raced to the nearest hospital; he had guessed right. He found Arthur in a real mess.

"He can't see anyone now, but he should be okay," the nurse assured him. "Come back in the morning."

William left, collected his shotgun from the house and rode straight to the watcher's house.

The red mist had engulfed him. Experience had taught him to strike while the iron was hot; the sooner, the better. They would never expect anything this quick and certainly would never believe what was going to happen. He parked, jumped over the fence and ran to the door. He did not knock. He shot the lock off and barged the door open into the room of shocked faces. It was a five-shot Browning shotgun. He asked no questions. He shot one knee of all four men in the room. As far as he was concerned, everyone was guilty. Four squealing men on the floor, he walked to the door and turned.

"You fucking amateurs watched us, but we watched you. We are always ahead of you fools. Next time you die, now you suffer. You have no idea what you are up against. You fucked up!"

He left on the bike. It all happened in a flash. It would take years for them to get over the shock, if ever. On his way home, he threw the gun onto Julian's latest site. It would be buried deep the next morning. "Job done, William," he said to himself. He failed to sleep; he just lay there, waiting for morning and his visit to Arthur. First, he needed to get Jane to speak to Angelina.

Chapter 12

Arthur was awake as he went in. He still looked very battered and distressed. He had broken ribs and a fractured cheekbone, plus numerous cuts.

"How are you feeling, Arthur?" William asked.

"Rough, but not as rough as the four men they brought in last night. Each one had a knee shot off. Please tell me it was not you, William."

"I will say nothing, Arthur, as I cannot lie to you."

"Jesus, William, this place was in uproar last night with it all. Nobody knows what happened. Someone suggested it was a local dispute."

"Well, you could call it that. Let's talk when we get you home, but now you stay here and rest up for the week. Tom will dispose of the truck, so there's no link to us. I am so relieved to see you, Arthur. I was worried sick. It could have been worse. I found the truck; they really went to town, didn't they?"

"Oh, yes. They did not hold back. Most of my damage was done by them and not in the accident," Arthur confirmed.

"Cowards. I knew I had to do something much worse and immediately. It will take them years to get over that."

"William, I am so glad we are on the same side."

"Arthur, we always will be. I love you, Arthur. Whatever you want, we will do; that is our strength. Total trust, brother ... Right, Arthur, you have sick leave. I will get back to work. I brought your phone charger so you can tell Angelina of your unfortunate accident. Is there anything you need? I forgot grapes!" William said, laughing lightly.

"I could do with a paper to read about any local events. That would be nice and interesting."

William went to buy him a couple of newspapers that featured the quadruple knee-capping mystery. Arthur had problems getting into a position to read the papers, but he managed. William left him giggling.

He smiled and waved goodbye. "See you later. I am going home for a wash."

William left and went to visit Jane. She looked cross.

"I called Angelina and played it down, but she is on her way here."

"Sorry, Jane, I was busy when Arthur had his accident."

"How is he?"

"He is on the mend; should be home by the weekend."

"Was it on the motorbike? Angelina told me what a racer he was."

"No, he was in the truck, and it was not his fault. I will be in later to see him and would like to see you after. Is that alright?"

"Yes, of course, but I can come and see him too."

"I will collect you from work. Perhaps you could call Angelina and find out when and where she will need picking up. Bye for now."

"Drive carefully. We do not want any more accidents."

William rode home with a lot on his mind; he had plenty to think about. He stopped to talk to Tom.

"Arthur crashed the truck; he is in hospital. I need a favour from you."

"Of course, name it."

"I want you to get rid of the truck. It's fucked anyway, but do not bring it back here."

"Understood, William. Take it from me; it is gone! How is Arthur?"

"He will be in hospital for the week, but he is on the mend. He is tough!"

"I have a feeling you are both tougher than we think, but both gentlemen. Leave it to me."

"Thanks, Tom. Oh, by the way, has Julian filled in that hole on his job yet?"

"Yes, all done." Tom smiled to himself. Whatever thoughts he was having, he cared not. Arthur and William's wellbeing was of great importance. The boys could rely totally on him and Julian.

William went to work, moving everything around, ready for the next and imminent harvest; life must go on. He worked hard while formulating a plan. 'When Arthur comes home,' thought William, 'we need to talk things over to consider options and a plan for the future'.

He finished work and prepared to visit the hospital. He walked across the yard and mounted the motorbike.

Tom wandered over. "Tell him we are thinking of him. And by the way, the gypsies have taken the truck. They gave me 200 euros for it for scrap." He held the money out to William.

"Keep it," William said. "That's yours for a good, prompt job. Thanks."

"If you are sure, William, I am very grateful. Have you read the paper? These four evil-looking shits got shot in the knees – all four of them. You can guarantee they deserved it; that was no accident. Someone did a proper job there."

"Looks like it, Tom."

He rode off to the hospital, where Arthur was already looking a bit better.

"Thank god you came, William. It is incredibly boring here."

"All is well at home. I will have harvested again before you get back. I came for a chat and then promised Jane she could come to see you. She was very upset. Have you spoken to Angelina yet?"

"No. I thought I would leave it for a few days not to worry her too soon."

"Okay, your call. Is there anything you want? I will go and get Jane."

"Anything to read – a motor magazine would be useful. I think we will need to change some of our vehicles."

"Our truck for a start," William said.

They both laughed.

"Oh, ow, that hurts. Don't make me laugh. My ribs can't take it."

William left and bought a selection of magazines. Jane was waiting for him outside work. He kissed her, smiled and said, "Ready then?"

"Yes, but I need to talk to you first. I rang Angelina. I knew he would not. You men ... She is coming on the train and will be at the station at eight tomorrow morning. Can you collect her?"

"Of course, I can, but you girls will have to take the blame, alright?"

"Yes. Some things you men have no idea about. He will be pleased, wait and see, but do not mention it to him. Leave it until she sees him. Promise?"

"I promise."

They were soon at his bedside.

"Arthur, how are you feeling?" Jane asked. "You must be more careful. William would be finished without you. How did it happen? Was the truck faulty?"

"No. I have no idea, but we needed a better one!"

She then noticed William was saying nothing, just leaving it all to Arthur. She changed the subject. "Are they feeding you alright?"

"Yes, the food is not bad. But I will soon be back and having to eat William's offerings, so hospital food is not that bad after all."

"Have you made any friends in here, Arthur?" Jane asked.

"No, but I might once I am back on my feet again."

"Do not rush it. Plenty of time for friends and acquaintances," William said, looking firmly into his eyes. "Anyway, choose us a new truck, if you can, and we will discuss it in the morning. Tom got the gypsies to collect the old one; we did not want it in the yard."

"Ah, that's good. You think of everything as usual, William."

Jane kissed him on the cheek, and William shook him firmly by the hand. Their handshakes meant as much and even more than any Mason's shake, and the square, unflinching eye-to-eye look meant even more.

"See you in the morning," William said. As they walked out, Jane's words to Arthur came to mind. "William could not manage without you." He found himself agreeing. 'No, I could not,' he thought to himself.

He stayed with Jane until late but could not settle. He made his excuses to leave.

Jane spoke as they were at the front door. "I do understand, William, and I know I will probably never know everything, will I? But that is okay. I am not a silly woman, and you mean the world to me, no matter what."

"Thank you, Jane. That is what I need, and you mean the world to me, too."

"Goodnight, sweetheart. See you tomorrow."

He spent another restless night.

William woke early and was well in time to collect Angelina from the station. She came smartly out carrying her overnight bag.

"Let us have coffee; it is early for the hospital yet," William said.

"Okay, then you can tell me all about it, ha ha ha. I know you won't, but I want you to know something, William. I understand the bond you two have, and I also know you both trust one another with your lives, so no matter what happened, it will not have been the fault of either of you. And if something needed to be done, it will have been. Neither of you need to tell me anything. All will be sorted satisfactorily."

"It has been, Angelina."

"Good, thank you, William. Now, no more talk. Let me see the man I love."

"He will be shocked, but will love to see you."

As they entered his room and approached Arthur's bed, William said, "Blame Jane."

But you could see Arthur blamed no one; he was so happy!

"Arthur, my love, thank goodness for Jane. You bloody secretive men!! I would still not know if it was not for her. I do not care about the whats, whys and wherefores; I just care that you – my man – is alright. I am staying in town with Jane until you are up and about, so do not argue."

"No, my love, I would not dare argue. I will enjoy having you around."

This was a very clever lady. She had already noticed the newspapers lying around and read the headlines. She missed nothing. She did not need to put two and two together; she went straight to four and four!! Four knees being rebuilt? Always going to limp badly!

"I will just go and get a coffee," Angelina said. "Do you two want anything? I won't be a minute." With that, she walked out of the door.

With the minimum of questions, she found her way to the ward of the four knee jobs. Angelina took out her phone, opened the door and took a photo of the four occupants. "I came from Paris today to make sure we have your pictures with no mistakes. One false move and a large part of France will be down on you like a ton of bricks. What I need now is a list of who you are working for."

"Don't worry; we are finished," one of them, seemingly the boss, replied. "We are leaving for Spain by the end of the week for our own safety. Friday is our last day. We will give you what you want to know then – before we disappear. We owe them nothing. They have cut us off already – even Jean here, who was a partner. There is no one all that important; they were just buyers and distributors."

"Friday, then. Don't forget. Are you being watched by your side?"

"No, they are too scared to show their faces anywhere near your Mr Fix It; he was unbelievable. No one will ever forget it; everyone is terrified – they've all gone into hiding."

"Yes, I should think so. We pay him enough, and he loves his job," she lied.

Angelina went back to Arthur. "Nice hospital, my love. I got lost, but now I know my way around, so tomorrow, I can visit on my own."

"Yes, my love."

Those words meant a lot to her. She looked at him with such compassion she welled up inside almost to bursting point. "Yes, Arthur. I do not want to worry or stress you, but I love you more than words can say. Now, William, take me to Jane's."

"Yes, ma'am, right now, ma'am. Tomorrow then, Arthur," William said.

"Yes. Tomorrow, William."

Not long after they left, she said, "Stop soon. We need to talk."

He stopped at a bar and ordered two beers.

"William, do you think that is the end of it?" Angelina asked.

"Yes, I hope so, but I will talk to them to make sure. They are actually in that hospital."

"Yes, I know. I have already spoken to them. It seems one was a partner, and the other three just hired assistants. All are terrified of you. I told them you are our gang's ultimate Mr Fix It. You do not talk; you are in the background as our ultimate deterrent. They are leaving on Friday, and they are giving me a list of who buys from them. In return, I said I'd guarantee their safe passage to Spain. I also told them I came down from head office in Paris to sort this out without involving you again, Mr Fix It, as you are very expensive. I hope I have done nothing wrong. I do not care what your business is, and if you like, I will say nothing to Jane. The only problem for you, William, is that I think Arthur might soon like to marry me, and I would jump at it if he ever asks."

"Angelina, one day he will tell you how we got together, but meanwhile, whatever Arthur wants, I will always agree to. I would love to see him happily married, more than likely to you. So whatever happens, let it happen. And yes, Jane deserves the truth. I will tell her very soon, but for the moment, I don't want to worry her. Also, Miss Arranger, I do think you handled the knee jobs well but don't say too much to Arthur yet. Lets' all get home for a week, then we can decide, okay?"

"Okay, Mr Well and Truly Fixed It."

"Hi, Jane. I can't thank you enough for calling me; these silly, secretive men!" Angelina said as Jane opened her front door to greet them.

"Yes, I know, but we love them all the same," Jane replied.

"Oh no, not you as well, Jane?"

"Yes, me too. Like it or lump it, it's the truth – the same as you and Arthur."

"I like it now that we all know."

"Okay, that is sorted then. Come in, Angelina, you must be worn out, and you, William, get back to work. I will call you tomorrow. Us girls will visit Arthur in the morning, alright?"

"Yes, sweetheart. I have work to do, and I have a feeling I will get some sleep tonight, thank goodness."

William rode off. Old habits die hard, so as usual, he took the long way home just in case. He stopped and started a few times but had no followers. When he got home, he did all the necessary jobs and arranged everything for the day's harvesting, which would start in the morning.

Chapter 13

William slept well and was ready for work early. By evening, half was done, and the rubbish had been dropped into the trailer outside the window. Everything else was hanging in the drying room. He would visit Arthur now and do the other half the next day.

As he left, Tom was outside. "All okay, William?"

"Yes, I have been busy, but I'm going to see Arthur now. He has had his lady with him all day, so I was *persona non grata* today."

"Good, I will go home now. Give him our regards."

"Sure, Tom. I will."

He opened Arthur's door. The girls were still there, fussing around him.

"Save me, William, save me!" Arthur said, holding his arms out to his friend and laughing.

"Take no notice, William; he loves the attention," Angelina said. "We will leave you two men alone for a while and have a proper meal. We will come back later to say goodnight."

William gave them a small wad of notes and said, "Treat yourselves, girls. We pay our nurses well."

"Thank you. We might be a bit late back." They both laughed and left.

After chatting generally for a while, Arthur asked, "How are things at home, William?"

"All okay. No problems, no strangers. I have done half the harvest, so I will finish tomorrow. Tom and Julian send their regards. Did you choose a car or a truck?"

"Sort of, but we will decide when I am back just in case of changes."

"Well, we have all the options. Most of our problems are slipping off to Spain as soon as possible. We will talk about that also when you are back. Right now, we have no problems, so get well and keep Angelina happy. Just one thing before they come back. Think about what suits you: carry on, have a change or move or retire. I will go with whatever you decide."

"Right, William. I will spend time thinking while I am in here, and then we will have a discussion."

"Yes, later then. I can see them coming back. Well, girls, did you dine well?"

"Yes, and we will go back to bed soon, and you, William, back to work. Arthur looks worn out; you should sleep well tonight."

They all left, but as William was leaving, he approached the night nurse. "Excuse me, I don't want to affect your other duties, but I will gladly pay you an extra 100 euros to watch over Arthur. Check he is alone and okay every ten or fifteen minutes."

"That's easy. I will turn the camera on to him and his door so that I can see him from in my office all the time. I did not like the looks of some of his injuries; they were too far apart to be from one accident. And I don't need your money."

"Give it to the hospital or a charity of your choice," William said.

"Well, thank you, kind sir. You can rely on me. I am Sian."

"Goodnight, Sian; I am William."

By the time he got home, he was ready for bed and slept like a log.

Morning came, and he was ready for work. He soon finished the harvest and dumped the trimmings and rubbish, which he set alight. Today, he would use the car again but still take the long way around. Arthur was getting better by the minute. He just had to be careful with his ribs for a few more weeks, but then, he would be as good as new. The girls visited him several times a day.

At the end of the week, Angelina went to see the four limpers. The boss gave her a paper with only three names on it.

"Two of these were my partners. The other one was just a helper, and that is it: no one of any consequences. All three live in Toulouse; the address is on there. Please leave us out of anything. I don't think they are capable of causing any problems for you. Their only strength is that they have money but no guts. Good luck. We are sorry for all this. Do not tell anyone where we have gone, please. We have plans for the very south of Spain."

"I believe you. If you have lied, Mr Fix It will find you easily – that is his job!"

"No lies, we promise."

They left under cover of darkness. William followed them and saw them board the Spanish train. He left the car near the van hire, drove the van home to the shed and loaded it ready for delivery to Adrian on the plateau in the morning.

On the way the following day, he collected from the hippy sites. Having done so, he made his way to the plateau. William transferred everything to Adrian's cross-country vehicle, got his payment with a grateful smile, and left for the roundabout journey to town. He quickly hid the money in the car and returned the hire van. He drove to the hospital. He left the car in sight of the ward windows, where it could be seen from Arthur's room where he was spending his last night of hospital. The girls were already there fussing around him.

"All done, Arthur, so it's a quiet day for us. I will come in the morning and have a late breakfast with the girls. Does that suit you, girls? I will see you here at 9 am. I expect Arthur will have to wait for the doctor to visit before he can leave, but he will be ready in good time."

He had to go home that night to remove the cash from the car and stash it away safely. This done, he visited the grow rooms. Everything was running nicely. In two more weeks' time, it would be ready to harvest again.

William slept like a log, but as usual, on the dot of seven, he was up getting his coffee. This was followed by a walk around the house with his eagle eye looking for any slight change or problem. As usual, all was checked and cleared before Tom and Julian arrived.

"Good morning, men. Any problems or anything you need? I have ordered a delivery of commercial diesel that should arrive today. I have left the business card on the office desk. The pin code is stuck on the bottom of my coffee mug in there, so one of you can pay when it arrives."

"That is trusting of you, boss," Tom said.

"Not really. All four of us trust one another – that is what our relationship is built on. I also hope I can trust you to come to me if you need help."

"Perfect, William. There is no situation where we would let either of you down, would we, Julian? This is like a family. Well, better than a family, in fact."

"Good. I am bringing Arthur home today, so if you are around late afternoon, perhaps we could have a few beers to welcome him."

"We will be here. Looking forward to seeing him."

William washed the car; after all, it had spent a lot of time in the shed. He drove to town and picked Jane up. Angelina was already at the hospital waiting for Arthur to have his final check and release. Jane went in to be with her and let her know that William was waiting in the car. Finally, they all came out, and William drove them to the restaurant where Jane worked. They would have a quiet lunch together. Arthur was already enjoying being outdoors and in the fresh air. Their table was ready outside but in the shade.

"This is perfect," Arthur exclaimed. "Lunch with my three best friends in the open air and no hurry. We can take all the time we want."

"Yes, Arthur, all the work at home is up to date – even some of the housework," William added, laughing.

They enjoyed half the day or more there. Then, as arranged, it was time for them all to go back to have a few beers with Tom and Julian. There was another surprise. As they drove into the yard, there was a 'Welcome Home' sign: crudely written but really appreciated. A home-made barbeque was also already alight. Tom and Julian had both got their wives with them. Arthur looked at William with a quizzical expression.

"I did not know, Arthur. They did all this for you!!"

"I do not care who did what, but I love it," Arthur said. "These two have proved to us over the last good while that they are a good, loyal family."

"Welcome, Boss and William," Tom joked, and everyone laughed.

Arthur responded, "This is great, boys, and it is about time we met your wives. Introduce me? No, I will introduce myself. Hello, ladies, welcome. It is so nice to meet you! And you came willingly? Wonderful," he laughed.

By now, all eight people were chatting like old best friends.

William was beaming. "If we had known you were all here, we would have come earlier. Let me get some more seats. We want to be comfortable, and we certainly do not want this to end soon."

"I will cook," Tom's wife said.

"And I will serve and mingle," Julian's wife offered.

William went into the house and came back with all sorts of seats, followed by a selection of bottles from the drinks cabinet, plus mugs and a few glasses. They all sat around the barbecue, chatting and laughing until the early hours. William was not a big drinker and had been careful; his ever-watchful nature helped in that.

At the end of the evening, he said, "Thanks, guys, for everything. Let us end on a safe note. I have not drunk much to make sure I can drive you all home." He took the four of them back to their houses, thanked them profusely, and then returned to Arthur and the girls.

"I can take you girls back in the morning. I will get you back in time for work, Jane."

"Yes, we would like to stay the night, wouldn't we, Angelina?"

"Yes. We are a bit concerned about the state of your rooms," Angelina said, laughing, "but we will take a chance."

"Tom and Julian obviously think a lot of you two, and their wives were really nice, too," Jane said.

"And very thoughtful," William added.

Chapter 14

They were up early. The weather was good, so they brought all the seats in again and cleared the yard.

"Shall we have breakfast before we take you to town? What time do you need to be back, Jane?" William asked.

"As long as I am there before eleven for work, it will be alright."

"Right, then. Let us have breakfast in the sun, then."

Halfway through coffee, Tom and Julian arrived for work and waved good morning. Angelina went over to thank them again, which they appreciated. The work day had begun. William arranged to take the girls to town, and all four sat in the sun in the square until Jane went to work.

"Well, Arthur, I will get back to work; I have a few things to do. You can entertain Angelina. I will only be a couple of hours or so. While I am away, both of you think about tomorrow. It is Jane's day off, and I thought we could all go to Andorra for the day. We always like a trip up the mountain, and the girls enjoy doing some shopping – Andorra is good for that."

"I will talk to Jane, then if she is happy, that is what we will do," Angelina said.

"Thanks, Angelina. I will see you later. Take it easy, Arthur."

"Yes, and you, William."

He drove back and entered the yard. Tom was busy and waved happily. William went straight into the grow rooms to organise it all. It would be ready again for harvest in one week. He checked the water and nutrient levels, also the automatic light settings. It was not hard work, but there were so many details to pay attention to and multiple repeat jobs to be remembered. These checked and rechecked, he locked up and went down for a sandwich. He made a few phone calls home to the UK, saying he was in Scotland. They could tell no difference as he used his WhatsApp mobile. Everything was quiet, so there was no need to return for another few months. William had just one more little job to do before collecting Arthur from town. He drove slowly out to the watcher's old house. He parked and walked purposefully around the area. The house was empty, with no sign of recent life. The door was crudely nailed shut, the lock still not repaired. The village itself was very quiet. William thought there would probably never be a reason to come here again. He drove a roundabout way back to town; old habits!!

His favourite trio were sitting and having a beer.

"I went back, finished my little jobs and rang the UK," William said. "All is quiet there, so everything is up to date. Now, what about tomorrow?"

"Well, I asked the girls, and they liked your idea of Andorra for the day," Arthur replied.

"Good. Shall we go back to our house for the night and make an early start in the morning? Do you need to pack anything, Jane?"

"Just a few things. Come with me, Angelina. I am sure these boys need a few moments to chat; you know how they are," Jane said, and they left.

"Well, any news, William?"

"All clear. I rang the UK and told them Scotland was good. Oxford is quiet, with no new faces. They asked when I would be back. I said I would let them know, but not for a month or two. I went round to the watcher's; it is empty and boarded up. We can enjoy tomorrow now without worry."

"Yes, I need that. Angelina has to go back to Paris this weekend."

"Well, we do not have to do much until after the weekend, anyway, so enjoy the now!"

Angelina and Jane came into sight, chatting and laughing; they had become close friends.

"Let us go back soon. We need to clean a bit and change the sheets before bedtime, boys!!!" Jane said.

"If you must," William replied.

"Yes, we must. I do not think you two have changed anything since you came to France, so today is the day, okay?"

"Alright, I suppose so," William said, then spoke quietly to Arthur. "Why do women enjoy cleaning things all the time?"

"I really do not know, but if it pleases them, let them do it."

When they arrived at the house, William and Arthur sat and watched the ladies change the bedding and clean the floors, a few chairs and tables. Now and then, both men lifted their feet to make way for brooms and the vacuum cleaner!

"Does this help you see what marriage would be like, William?" Arthur asked.

"Yes," he laughed, "it makes me think danger! Danger!"

It was time for bed. The boys handed the girls the obligatory glass of water. All tired, they were all asleep within half an hour.

It was an early breakfast, with the girls more eager than the boys to get to Andorra and, of course, the shops. Outside, Tom and Julian were busying themselves in the yard.

"Tom, Julian, we are going to Andorra," William announced. "Do you want anything? Tobacco or alcohol?"

"Yes, please," Tom answered, and they both quickly wrote down their needs.

"Okay, we will manage that. See you later."

With William driving, they were off. Arthur's ribs were still a bit delicate for him to drive that trip when it was unnecessary. They stopped twice on the way to take in the view and for refreshments. They had all day, so there was no rush.

Once parked, for the girls, it became more hurried and a quickening of step to the shops. The boys had provided them with plenty of cash so they would not be needed until lunchtime, which was arranged for one o'clock at the Piste restaurant. The boys had their own appointment with Adrian at his shop. This was not only to buy the tobacco and alcohol they needed, including for Tom and Julian, but also a social meeting to show appreciation for the business they had established with Adrian on the plateau every couple of weeks.

"Hi, Adrian. Good to see you. Is everything okay at this end? Any problems?" William asked.

"No, all's quiet and sensible here," Adrian replied.

"That's good to hear. We all just want a quiet life, after all, until some greedy idiot tries to fuck it up."

"We needed to do some shopping and have brought our ladies with us for a treat day out. They know nothing of our business and don't know of you at all, but if you and your lady wife would like to join us for lunch, it would be our treat. We would like to introduce you as our friend and shopkeeper that we always buy our tobacco and alcohol from. If you can make it, please do. We will be at the Piste restaurant from one o'clock onwards."

"Okay, I would love to come, and my wife loves to eat out and says I should make more effort. I know she will say yes!"

"Good, we will wander on and hope to see you later with her."

It was not hard finding their ladies. Typically, once in a good department store, they were slow-moving, checking everything and chatting happily.

"Hey, girls. All okay?"

"Yes. What about you two?"

"Yes, we are finished. We will put what we have in the car now and have coffee somewhere. Have you much to take to the car yet?"

"Yes, these few bags here. Not much, if you don't mind taking them."

"Right, I think us two can manage those few bags!" William said. "We will see you at the Piste. We've booked a table for six people for one o'clock. We have two friends for you to meet. Don't be late if you can help it."

The girls probably worked hard at shopping, and the boys relaxed and enjoyed their freedom.

Lunchtime came, and all four were meeting outside the Piste. Adrian was already inside with his wife, Mali.

"Ah, great, Adrian. You made it. I am so glad," William said as they entered the restaurant.

"We are looking forward to it. This is my wife, Mali."

"Nice to meet you, Mali ."

They all introduced themselves and were taken to the best table.

"We are so glad you chose it here. It's my wife's favourite. We also know the owner, so good news all round."

Arthur joined in with the proceedings. "What would you all like to drink?"

They all seemed happier with the social meeting and event than with what to drink. They all initially wanted water with the meal, then coffee and alcohol. After all, the main thing for everyone was that easy, happy atmosphere between good friends, which was naturally happening. This could be a long, comfortable lunch.

It was well into the afternoon when they broke up.

Jane spoke for them all. "That was really nice. I feel we will all be close friends from now on.

William and I have the knack for making friends with perfect and similar people, so thanks, all of you. We should do this again soon or meet up regularly, at least."

Adrian and Mali went back to the shop, and the others to do a last round of the town shops. All were feeling a good deal slower after the heavy lunch, but there was no need to hurry. Soon, Angelina would have to go back to Paris, and Jane would find as the summer holidays were ending, she would no longer have her job.

It was dark before they managed to wrench themselves away from Andorra. It was a quiet but smiley journey back. The music had been ideal on the radio and now acted like a magnet. Even when they arrived at the house, all four just sat listening and not attempting to get out of the car or switch off.

"Well, I suppose we should go in and get our beauty sleep – especially William," Arthur said.

They all laughed, went in and straight to bed in their now clean bedrooms!!

Chapter 15

At breakfast time, Jane made the coffee and toast. No one was really hungry, but it was very welcome. Arthur took the box of goodies out to Tom and Julian.

"Good morning, guys. Here is your delivery from Andorra. We added some wine and bottles of Baileys for your wives. I hope we chose right."

"How much, Boss?" Tom asked.

"No charge. It's all yours. Enjoy. For your loyalty."

"Hey, thanks a million. We did not expect that."

"You deserve it. I think we chose right for the ladies. We remembered what they liked at the party."

"They will be more than happy. They love being included. Anyway, how are you now? Are your ribs comfortable?"

"Getting better every day. Another week and I will be back to normal, and Doctor William will have no need to fuss around me like a mother hen."

"Well, I would not mind a mother hen like him watching out for me."

"No, I have no complaints. One day I will explain how we got together. It started practically the same as he is now: very thoughtful, very loyal and very strong, but most of all, a man of his word. If he says something, he will do it – he's unstoppable!!!! Anyway, you two, enjoy your tobacco. I will get back to breakfast. Have a good day," Arthur said and went back to his coffee.

"This weekend, Arthur, are you going to be up to driving Angelina back to Paris?" William asked. "She says she will go on the train if not."

"What if I go on the train with her? I quite fancy the idea; then we can get a taxi to her house. It's got to be easier and we get to spend another day together."

"Right, that is settled then. What are you girls doing today?"

"I have to be at work at 11 am," Jane replied, "then I'm busy until late, so today, I think Angelina should stay here with Arthur."

"We will take you in at 11, then stay for lunch. The three of us will come back after to work. Then all come in in the evening to be with you. All agreed? Angelina can sit in the garden or clean a bit while we attend to work."

They drove Jane to town, and it was soon lunchtime. As usual, to please Jane's boss, they had lunch with her there.

All too soon, they were back in the yard.

"Angelina, look after Arthur," William said. "Don't let him do too much. I can manage."

Without the boys knowing, Jane and Angelina had bought bedding and towels in Andorra, along with cleaning fluids. This was much appreciated by the boys, although they had not wanted them to spend anything other than on themselves. Angelina was soon cleaning and changing things, which left Arthur to help William with the harvest. The timing of this was right, and between the two of them, everything was soon trimmed and hung to dry. One week later, it would be ready for delivery to Adrian when Arthur got back from Paris.

Once more, William was quietly thinking all was going too well and smoothly. 'Look out,

William, it can't last forever!!' he thought to himself.

By the time they drove to town for their evening meal with Jane, she was very pleased to see them and even happier to come back to the house with them for the night. Angelina had already told her she had fitted the new bedding and cleaned both rooms a bit.

Once home, they were all soon in bed and asleep. The plan for the next day was the same, other than checking train times and buying tickets for the weekend.

When it was time to go, it showed on Angelina's face just how much this place had become a home to her, with all the cleaning and organising she had done. But mainly, she had become even closer to Arthur; they would both miss one another badly, even for a day or so. It would be a happy trip to Paris but a very lonely one back. At least when he got back, there was plenty of work to be done to keep his mind occupied.

On Arthur's return, the harvest was dry enough, so they weighed and bagged it, ready for delivery to Adrian. Now feeling much fitter, Arthur had collected from the hippies and met with William to give him those bags, along with their own, for him to take to the plateau. All went as arranged.

One cloud on the horizon was that the story of the four knee-cappings was all over the English papers and had attracted the gang's attention. Still bearing a grudge, they were busily discussing the possibility of it being William, here in the south of France, not in Scotland as they originally thought.

"We should get someone to check it out; you never know!! That William is a cunning bastard capable of anything!!!! I will not rest until I have him in my grasp!!!!!" was heard several times by a number of interested parties. Word started to filter back to France.

Four limping drug dealing friends in Spain were not hard to find, and when approached, although not happy to say much, it was clear they would need to search the south of France area for "the fixer" and hope it would turn out to be William. So the French village house of the shootings was the next place to go on their search. Whether it was William, the fixer, or both, they had learned enough to be extremely careful. They had plenty of time.

"Let us head to the nearest town and see who knows anything," the group leader said. "Don't make it obvious. We enter separately and casually to ask where we can buy some weed and go from there."

After a few towns, they had still found nothing. No one knew of any dealers. Some had heard about the shootings but knew nothing about who could possibly have been involved. The only thing to go on was an old picture of William. It looked as though they would have to use it and ask directly if anyone knew or had seen him. That was the dangerous option, but they needed to try.

"We will have to draw lots to see which of us does the asking. It has to be a low-key, casual thing."

It still remained a problem where to start and which towns to start in.

"Let's try the nearest to the shooting house and work outwards."

It was inevitable that someone would think they recognised him. Someone did and also linked him to Jane.

"I think he is the boyfriend of the girl at that restaurant. Try asking her," one of the neighbours said.

Well, they would not approach her but would watch her and wait to see her boyfriend.

William was busy, and Arthur was away for two days, taking Angelina back to Paris on the train. Luckily, William was preparing the next delivery and collecting from the hippies in time for Arthur to help deliver to Adrian on the plateau. All was ready on time, and William called Arthur.

"When will you be at the station? I will pick you up."

"Tonight at ten. Is that alright?"

"Yes, sure, I will be there; then, in the morning, we can load the van I've hired and deliver."

William was waiting at the station, and Arthur arrived on time. They went straight home to load for the morning.

William phoned Jane. "Are you okay, Jane?"

"Yes. Where are you?"

"I am at home with Arthur. We are working in the morning, then will come to see you at lunchtime."

"By the way, William, there is a strange man hanging around here. He is over the road at the bar with two others. They seem to be up to something, but most of the time, they're making out that they don't know one another. This one was friendly. He asked if I had a boyfriend, how often I saw him and if it was serious. He has asked nothing else, but he is still around, and they're definitely not holidaymakers."

"Act dumb, Jane. Say nothing. I will ring in the morning before I come in for an update, just in case. Be careful. Love you."

"Love you, too, my Willy."

William had been expecting something. He had hired the van and kept out of the town centre, so he had probably not been spotted. It was also lucky he had not visited Jane before collecting Arthur.

"You are looking worried, William," Arthur observed.

"Yes. Jane has had someone asking after me, then meeting with two others in the bar opposite. I think they are on to me!"

"Well, it was bound to happen, William. What's the plan? Have you got one yet?"

"Not yet. First, we deliver in the morning and tidy up any loose ends. Let's sleep now and make an early start."

It was an early start, too, and an early start for the hippies and Adrian, but so far, so good. All was delivered and paid for, and finally, the cash was stowed away.

"Now we have decisions to make," William said. "We could disappear for a while, but I don't like leaving Jane to face any music if there is any. They have an idea she is my girlfriend, and they may use that to get to me. I could fix all three but be vulnerable, and then the cat would be out of the bag, and I might have to face all hell from England. Arthur, the way I see it is, as they have not yet seen me, to be sure, what if I go to England via Scotland tomorrow? Jane could end her job two weeks early and go home to her old village and family; I will pay her the extra. You carry on quietly without delivering. You sign over the yard to Tom and Adrian as a barrier to the house and a safeguard for them and their business. While in England, I will sell the garage and workshops.

That will pretty well guarantee I am seen there. Do you think this is enough to make them leave here and go without any final event?"

"I don't know," Arthur replied, "but you will have to explain to Jane."

"Yes, I know. Now, a question for you, Arthur. How close are you to Angelina?"

"Very."

"Is she the one, Arthur?"

"Yes."

"One last question. Where would you like to live, and what would you like to do? I presume you're like me – I need a goal or job. Well, I am going to call Jane now, and then you and I will talk."

"William, they are still hanging around," Jane said.

"Can you resign early?"

"Yes."

"If I send you a package, where would you like to go for a month? I have to go back to the UK to cover my tracks."

"I have spoken to Angelina, and she wanted me to go to her when my job finished."

"My past is catching up with me. I need you safe while I go and check things out. I don't think you would be in any danger, but I need to feel free to do the necessary without worrying about anyone else."

"William, I fully understand. I will resign tonight. They will not be surprised. Plus, the holidays are finishing, and business has dropped off, so it will suit them. I will take a taxi to the station."

"I will be there on the motorbike at 9 am for our *Au revoir.*"

"I will tell my boss at the restaurant I have fallen out with you, which is why I am going early – just in case they get asked what happened to me. Is that alright with you?"

"Yes, and I will avoid them from now on!"

"See you in the morning then, sweetheart."

Chapter 16

It went as planned. William rode up to her at the station and handed her a parcel. Jane tried to refuse, but he insisted, and she was persuaded to take it. Most of the time, he kept his helmet on as a sort of disguise.

"I do love you, Jane."

"Please be careful, William. I need you. I will wait with Angelina in Paris. Please, William, no silly chances!!"

"It will be alright, Jane. I am very careful, and I have Arthur."

"Bye, William," Jane said. She was crying as she got on the train.

"Soon, Jane. Love to Angelina. Arthur will be in touch with her all the time."

The train pulled out, and William rode off. Having taken another route back, he rode into the yard, waved to Tom and went into Arthur.

"She went, Arthur. Half a day, and those girls will be together."

"I like the idea of that."

"Me too. Now, bring it on; the sooner, the better. Tomorrow, we'll go to the solicitors with Tom and Julian. I've made an appointment, and the papers are in my case, ready. I will talk to Tom now and get him ready with Julian."

Straight after breakfast, they were all in the car.

"What's this all about, William?"

"Arthur and me have decided to sign the yard over to you two as partners: half each. What we need from you is a handshake agreeing that you will run it as your business for at least five years. It will help us that you will see anyone coming and going. Just keep us informed; no need for anything else. We might come and go from the house, but we won't be living here often anymore. The girls have left here, so eventually, we will live with them somewhere else. Now, we want you to be secure, and that will help us.

"On the black side, our past is catching up with us." Arthur took over. "There are three men in town looking for William. He is going back to the UK as a diversion, and he will tidy up loose ends there."

"We could, of course, steam in and take them on, and we still might have to, but that would only mean others would come," William said. "This way, the girls are safe, and you two will be separate and secure, so if we have to go, there will be no leads or attachments here for anyone to use. Anyway, the lawyer will explain that without knowing why. The yard is now yours, lock, stock and barrel. Good luck, Tom; good luck, Julian!!!!"

"Well, good luck to you two. Here is my hand; if you need anything, just ask," Arthur said.

"Mine, too, Boss, and good luck. We know you are not angels, but to us, you are gentlemen and always will be."

They all shook hands and spent an hour with the lawyers. They came out very happy and shook again.

"Arthur, as soon as you have any more number plates for us to watch out for, please let us have them," Tom said.

"We will," William replied. "Also, while I am away in the UK, we want you to be observant, as Arthur will be here on his own for a while. At the moment, they have no idea where either of us lives, but just in case they stumble on something, it's best to be aware. But don't get involved because we need you here and not connected to us, okay?"

"Understood! We will get back to work, and thanks both. Thanks a lot; we won't forget it."

William booked his no-frills flight to Scotland, and Arthur took him to the airport. "Arthur, I will be back in a week or so if you can stay away from town. When I get back, you will be ready for a delivery. After that and what happens in the UK, when I am there, we will make our plan. Till then, please lie low. Tom will do any shopping you need!" He waved and headed through security before going to board the plane.

Two hours later, he landed in Scotland, and the train was close by. He stuck Scottish stickers on his empty case, got on and found a seat to get comfortable for the journey south. He was half-way back already. He had arranged a hire car in Oxford, again close to the station. It wasn't until he was in the car that he started to feel anxious. He drove straight to the estate agent and put the garage on the market at an attractive price. He mentioned that the sitting tenants would probably like to buy. William then walked to the lawyer's office on the same road. He signed over power of attorney to them in case he was not there when it was sold. He also left the bank details for the money to be banked. Now he would visit the site and talk to the current renters. He was pretty sure they would like to buy it, particularly at the price he was asking.

The deal was done, and they shook hands. He informed the agent. All the formalities were arranged quickly, but payment and legal papers would not be ready for a month, possibly two. There was nothing more he could do. Now he needed to sort out the personal problems, which meant he would have to have contact with the local gang. He was not looking forward to that, but it had to be done. He was sure he had been seen since he got back. Now he must make sure any meeting was on his direction and terms. When the time came, he wanted as many aces in his hands as possible. He knew where a local crook/friend had a gun hidden. It was time to get it, although there would be no circumstances where he would be wise to use it. As a deterrent, yes, but in anger, no. That would only lead to making matters worse. For now, he had booked into a cheap motel. He had two rooms in the hope of confusing anyone, booked under different names, of course.

It was not long before he was approached. A friendly enough man was sitting on a seat close to his hire car. "Hello, William, it's been a long time. Where have you been?" The man was not expecting an answer.

"Working," replied William.

"Can we have a talk?"

"Okay, but I doubt if I can help you."

"Ah, yes, you can. I am sure you can. You see, firstly, you were the last person seen to be dealing with Raj, and secondly, this London mob don't seem to exist – it was one of your inventions. And lastly, you ran rather than answered. Only a guilty man runs, and you have been gone for three or four years!"

"I did not run but just moved my business to somewhere safe before the wrong type of person found it, so no mystery there; just normal behaviour. As for the London mob, they were here, but once I was gone, there was nothing, well, very little, to hang around for. Your lot had turned up and half-killed me trying to find out what I did not know when Jock turned up, kicked your gang's asses and advised me to disappear. What was the point of me staying, or the London mob, for that matter? Certainly not profit. Anyway, what do you want from me now?"

"The same thing. Where is Raj? What happened to him?"

"Well, I don't know, and even if I did, you wouldn't be happy. The only thing you want is vengeance, for one reason or another. So whatever I do or don't know, it will never be enough for your boss. He possibly sees me as a threat, whereas the best thing for all of us to do is to forget Raj and get on in peace and quiet."

"No, William. It has gone on too long now. My chief wants satisfaction. Raj was his brother, and he disappeared in the middle of talking to you. The last thing anyone saw of him was you taking him off, never to be seen again. Don't mess around; there is no way out of it. You have to give them something, and also, where is the man who saved you?"

"Jock did his thing. He owed a debt, so he paid it and left me, as I am sure you know, in hospital, where I was not going to stay for you to have another go!"

"You keep saying me, but it is not me, William. I don't care whether you live or die. But my bosses, and there are a lot of them, will not give up. My job is done. I have spoken to you. Unless you have a radical suggestion, I have to report back to them. And leave it to them when and how they finish it. You have been here nearly a week and have met no one of any consequence. My advice to you is to disappear soon, or they will make you disappear in a way that suits them."

"I am going nowhere. It would be to their advantage to talk to me."

"Well, William, I will tell them, but I don't think they will bother to talk. I am afraid you are done for."

William went back to his room, where he noticed his case had been moved – only slightly, but moved. There was not much in it, but he suspected the Scotland stickers, small though they were, would have been seen but possibly not believed! What now? He needed to think fast. There was no point in waiting around as, one way or another, his end would come eventually. So firstly, he needed to move on without being followed. So far, he had not used his phone here. It was time to destroy it as, in the wrong hands, it would supply the names and numbers of everyone in France and the UK. He took it to bits, wrecked the card and phone and ditched the parts. At some point, he would have to buy another, but not now or here. Case in hand, he boarded the train to Scotland. As usual, he put the case on the rack at the end of the carriage and went back to his seat. He settled in. Half an hour later, he got up, walked to the toilet situated between the carriages, and then slowly back to his seat. He bought a coffee at the first opportunity and slowly drank it. He also ate a sandwich. All the time, he had a feeling he was being watched, but even if he was, it would be no surprise. When he got up again to visit the toilet, he waited by the toilet door until the train was about to leave. It was polite to refrain from using the toilet until it left the station, but this time, as the train started, he jumped out just before the door closed, unseen, he hoped. Anyone watching was probably watching his case that he now had abandoned. Being double cautious, he got a taxi and instructed the driver to take him to the bus station so he could catch a bus to Scotland. But, of course, after entering the bus station, he went out of the side door and caught another taxi to the next town. Then he took a bus to Stanstead airport and bought a ticket to Barcelona. Once there, he would buy another phone to call Arthur.

Chapter 17

The trip was uneventful. William did wonder when they finally realised he was no longer on the train. If, as William thought, they had secreted a tracker on his case, they would probably follow it to its eventual home in lost luggage. And if they had realised when he got off the train, there were more false trails involving buses and taxis. After that, it was very unlikely they would know what to do, let alone fly to Barcelona.

William had some business to see to on the coast, including some properties to look at for future reference. This done, he caught the train up to Andorra. It was a pleasant trip from the Spanish side, and always good to meet up with Adrian, who was only too pleased to supply William with a new phone. Now, he could talk to Arthur.

"Hi, Arthur. How are things there with you?"

"All very quiet, but then I haven't left the house. Tom did some shopping for me, and I have worked solidly all the while you have been away.

I now know how hard you have worked while I have been out of it, in hospital and to Paris a few times."

"No problem, Arthur. As you are probably finding, when you are alone, work easily comes first and is welcome."

"Where are you?"

"Well, I think it's better for you to guess, but I will need you to collect me from our favourite restaurant where the six of us ate last time."

"Okay, now I know where, but when and what time?"

"Tomorrow at midday, if that is alright with you?"

"Perfect. I could do with a run out."

"By the way, take note of this number. It's my new phone."

Next, William rang Jane. "Hi, sweetheart. Are you okay?"

"Of course not, and I never will be without you, William. I have been so worried," she replied.

"I am perfectly alright. I took a long way round to get back and had to ditch my old phone. This is a new one. I tied up the loose ends in the UK and won't have to go back again. I love you, Jane. How is Angelina?"

"She is great but longing to see Arthur. I think they want to make plans – if you know what I mean."

"Yes, I thought as much. What about you, Jane? Are you wanting to make plans?"

"It takes two, William, so I don't know."

"We will make plans soon, then."

"I would love that if possible."

"Another few weeks, and we will be free to. Bye, for now, sweetheart."

William ended the call and walked round to Adrian's shop. Adrian saw him coming and ran outside.

"Hey, William! This is unexpected."

"Yes, I have been back to the UK, but I took the long way back through Barcelona. Arthur is collecting me soon. How are things going with you?"

"All good, no problems. In fact, we are due to meet in two days' time."

"Yes, all is on its way. I spoke to Arthur; he is nearly ready, so we will meet as usual. Also, Adrian, I was wondering, do you have a clean, honest friend or family member to train up? We have an anonymous site registered to us that produces a lot – all automatic. On paper, it is rented to whoever, so if ever there was a problem, they could just walk away and not be traced, leaving us bewildered as to what was happening. At some time or other, Arthur and me will also have to walk away: me, for safety reasons. I am a known face to a bigger opposition. Arthur is clean, but I am always worried someone might recognise me and ruin a whole business link, and I am belt and braces!!! Safety first."

"I understand. I will think about it. I do have a few ideas of people I am already involved with. I will let you know," Adrian responded.

"Okay, no hurry. To make it easier, we could, for a while, collect a reasonable rent and keep an eye on everything."

"Sounds good to me, but we will talk again at our next meet on the plateau."

"Until something is sorted, business as usual, then. Arthur will be here soon. Have a beer with us; then we will go home and see you the day after tomorrow. We will sort out the finer details then."

"I can see Arthur now," Adrian said, "so a beer or dinner now. Which suits you?"

"Wait. I will ask Arthur, but knowing him, it will be dinner. He always wants to eat, and he hasn't been out for two weeks. I am willing to bet he has not cooked once. Adrian, fetch your wife. Let's all eat together."

"Good idea. We will meet you at the Piste; I know she will love it."

William and Arthur greeted one another warmly, headed to the restaurant and found a table. Adrian arrived with his wife. As predicted, Arthur was very hungry. "Do we need anything for home food-wise, Arthur?"

"No, we have everything we need, and Tom did some shopping for me in the week."

They were soon on the way back. It was already dark, and both were tired and ready for bed by the time they got to the house.

"Tomorrow, we will talk, Arthur. Things have escalated back home, but I have sold the garages. Final signing is in a month, so there's no need for me to go back. I need a good sleep tonight; then, after breakfast, we will go through the options. You know me; I always have or need a plan."

"Yes, William. I have come to rely on it. Goodnight, pal."

"Goodnight."

They slept well but were still up early for work.

"Straight after breakfast, we should finish packing and weighing, ready to deliver," William said.

"It's all done, William. Just needs a bit of reorganising, ready for the next harvest, and we can spend time sorting everything out."

"What is happening with the three men in town? Are they getting any closer?"

"They spend every day going from town to town asking about growers and dealers. It's a wonder no one has had a go at them. The best thing is you predicted it was imperative not to deal anywhere local, and it's all sold in one go now. As it has turned out, the watchers' team were got rid of, so now there are no connections within one hundred kilometres. If we have to have a confrontation, then it needs to happen at least two hundred kilometres away, preferably east and near a large town like Toulouse. Then, if there is a lead left, it will be way away from here," Arthur said.

"Limoges is a lot further, and there is a lot of wild countryside that way – all very handy for unseen action. Have Tom and Julian arrived yet? I need a quick word." William wandered out to see if he could find them.

"Good morning, Tom. All okay?" William asked.

"Yes, all good, but we both have seen the car with the number plate you gave us in town. As far as we know, it has not been any nearer."

"No matter what anyone asks, you two are the owners and don't know of anyone else around."

"Yes, we know the form."

"Good. One other thing. Julian, can you dig a hole in the bottom of the garden by the fence? Big enough for a swimming pool. No hurry, but this week if possible."

"Leave it to me," Julian replied.

"Thanks, Julian."

William went back to Arthur. "An hour or so and we will be done here for the day. How is Angelina?"

"Good. A bit anxious at being stuck in Paris, but she is enjoying Jane's company."

"Would you like to marry her, Arthur?"

"Well, yes, but it sounds as though you have a plan. Tell me what you are thinking."

"You are right. Of course, I have a plan, but as usual, I need your agreement first. As you know, I sold the garage, and the cash will be in the bank in a month. While I was in Barcelona, I visited the coast to see a hotel for sale. Property is still cheap there, and people with enough cash to buy something big like that are scarce. I have shown interest in it, and what I thought was if we bought it, we could put it in the girls' names for their security and also so that there would be no link to us. We could be with them as much as we liked, if not all the time. They would have an income, and we could have wives, that is if we wanted," he added, laughing.

"William, I think you have done it again. I know for certain it is what Jane and Angelina want."

"And you, Arthur?"

"Yes, William, and I am sure it's what you want, too; otherwise, you wouldn't have suggested it."

"Right I will show you on the laptop to see what you think. Then, in the week, we can visit it and make an offer. Let's hire a van from Toulouse. Best not to keep using the same place. Also, we should not go into town more than strictly necessary."

"William, you stay here. I will collect the van right now. It's probably best if we are never seen together unless absolutely necessary."

"Thanks, Arthur. I have done too much travelling lately."

As usual, William had busied himself every moment while Arthur was away collecting the van. As soon as he was back, it was loaded for the next day's delivery.

"Everything in the grow rooms is up to date and running well, so we can get away as soon as we want in the morning," William said.

They both spoke to the girls that evening but stopped themselves from mentioning Spain and living together. There were several bridges to cross first.

Chapter 18

They left the next morning, following the same rules: William in the van and Arthur on the motorbike as trail finder, checking for problems. William collected from the hippies and was on the plateau within the hour, meeting Adrian.

"Any thoughts, Adrian?"

"Yes, I am almost certain, and I like the idea. Just one problem: delivery! No one wants to deliver – it could be dangerous."

"No problem, we can still do deliveries. After all, we have other places to collect from. Possibly for 15 per cent, we would collect and deliver every month. What about something like that?"

"That sounds alright. Let's talk again at the next delivery. We can tie it all up then."

William took the cash back while Arthur took the van to Toulouse and then came home again in the car.

"From now on, Arthur, I will use Limoges and be seen there on my own. I need them to think I am a lone wolf. I am never ever going to shake them off any other way. I will arrange a confrontation: a bad and final one. I can't ever be seen with anyone else. I have to finish this on my own."

"William, this needs to be the best plan you have ever come up with. It will be a matter of life and death."

"I know, and that is another reason I want to provide for Jane in case something happens to me, well and the same for all of you. A way to retreat in safety and comfort. Tomorrow, let us go to Spain, check the hotel out and perhaps see a few others. Let's go early – straight after breakfast."

They left early to get this next step started. They liked three different properties: a minimum of ten rooms, a large dining room and a pool bar.

"I could live in any of them, William," Arthur said.

"Yes, and all three, if run properly, could be profitable and productive. They are all big enough to justify staff and make a good income. I think our next move should be to make three cheeky offers and then decide."

"Which one do you think is most suitable? I prefer number one," Arthur declared.

"Yes, number one for me, too. So, a really low price for the other two and see what happens."

Less than a week had passed when they heard that all three offers had been accepted, so naturally, they chose number one and paid the deposit immediately.

"When do we tell the girls?" Arthur asked.

"As soon as you like. We will need them to look it over and, of course, bring their passports because it is vital it gets put in their names legally."

"I will ring Angelina tonight, and she and Jane can have a long sort-out chat, ready for their visit. After all, it has got to suit both of them."

Arthur spoke to Angelina, who sounded ecstatic. By the time William spoke to Jane, the cat was well and truly out of the bag, and she was in shock and worried.

"William, are you okay? Are you still in danger? That's what concerns me most. The hotel is great, but not without you."

"I am okay, just sorting things out, and this will help me be anonymous and out of harm's way. Anyway, your security is of paramount concern to me. As soon as you can come, let us know, and we will take you to get your approval. Don't forget your passports and any personal papers. I am longing to see you."

"Angelina has just told me we should come on the train in the morning. Can you collect us from the station at 11 am tomorrow? Then we should be able to see the property in the afternoon. So, my love, 11 am – don't be late!!!!"

"One of us will be there waiting. So tomorrow, my love, *mañana, mañana.*"

Of course, it was Arthur who went to the station; William could not take the chance of being seen. Even though the three men appeared to have moved on for now, the boys were not about to take chances until it suited them.

Arthur drove the girls to the meeting point halfway to Barcelona, where they picked William up.

"I spoke to the agent," William updated them all. "He is going to meet us at our number one choice so we can get started straight away and spend as long as we like there."

As they pulled up outside the hotel, it was a warm day, and the high tide meant the sea was practically up to the building. The hotel was not massive, but it was imposing.

"Well," said Jane, "it's so much better than I imagined. What do you think, Angie?"

"I'm gobsmacked. Where do I sign?" she joked.

They went in and proceeded to inspect everything. Some furniture and the kitchen needed upgrading, but on the whole, it was good: it had been looked after.

"It needs some decorating, Arthur," William said.

"Yes, but that is all, and we knocked the price down, so we can afford it."

"Yes, we can do everything today. It will be a month before we can move in with all the legalities, but that will soon pass. Our last question, girls. Do you like the idea of the business? Will you be happy with it?"

Both girls, in unison, said, "Yes, yes, yes!"

"I can't wait, can you, Jane?" Angelina asked.

"No! I don't think I will be able to sleep until we are all in together."

"Let's go to the agents and then the lawyers. We can get it all done now, today, including the insurance. You have both got your passports, haven't you?"

Of course, they had. The formalities were finished at the agents, and the appointment at the lawyer's office was arranged for 2 pm. That took another hour, but a satisfying hour!

"Well, girls. Another thing to think about is the name. A new business needs a new name. You have a month to decide, but I can give you a couple of suggestions that might help. Both are a combination of your names. The first is JANGLES, as in Bojangles; the other ANGELS. I am sure there are a lot of others, and you two need to choose, but those could start the ball rolling."

"Let's eat here, William," Arthur suggested. "We can get a feel for the town and look around some more. We can take a few measurements for curtains and mats and a few upgraded pieces of furniture."

"If you like, we can stay the night and leave after breakfast. We will still be back by midday.

Unfortunately, girls, we will need to put you on the Paris train the following day as we have work to do and loose ends to tie up as soon as possible."

"Are you two going to retire then, William?" Angelina asked.

"We are cutting back a lot, but perhaps not completely yet. But yes, big changes after. We are soon going to be kept men – kept by wealthy land ladies," William added, laughing.

"Everything we do from now on is aimed at retirement – quietly, of course, isn't it, William?"

"Yes, I am sure we will find interesting things to do, Arthur. Pastures new – onward and upward."

It was getting closer now for William and Arthur: the peaceful, happy life! But, as usual, in the back of William's mind, as experience had told him, was that something could so easily go wrong. And having gone through easier quiet times, he felt a large foreboding. Something could so easily go wrong to ruin it all at the last moment. Even Arthur had started to have worrying thoughts, and he was usually the eternal optimist.

The town felt like home. The area was relaxing for all of them. On the way back, the car was full of happy banter. The girls were very happy but quietly sad at the thought of being put back on the Paris train for now. It all came around too soon. The boys worked away alone again while formulating a plan that would get the opposition permanently.

Off the scent without William meeting his end, he had a plan which he shared with Arthur. "As soon as we are up to date with our work here, I need to be seen in Limoges and that area. I need to attract them there because any confrontation needs to be there and far away from here. First, I need to find some growers to be seen to deal with, perhaps offering my services as Mr Fix It – casually, of course. Most of these little teams talk a lot. I don't think it will take long for it to filter to the opposition. At the moment, we don't know where they are. The only other option would be to lie low forever, but all hell could break loose when we least expect it and where we don't want it. So I think we have to push it and choose our own ground.

"There is an old Mercedes for sale on the Toulouse road. I will buy it and start using it in and around Limoges. It should attract the attention needed and also have no connection to anywhere around here. And if, as I expect, it gets damaged while they try to damage me, then it won't be missed. I won't insure it either. Arthur, I am going to Limoges to get noticed, of course, with my Mercedes. We don't have to deliver for two weeks, so now is a good time."

William drove to the outskirts of Limoges, visited a couple of the scruffier bars and casually brought up the subject of cannabis. It was easy to find some to buy, but a different matter to find where it was being grown in any quantity. Still, the main purpose for being around was to make his presence felt and gain attention, albeit not too blatantly. He asked at one bar about the chance of bulk buying.

"Well, I will inquire and let you know soon," one obvious dealer had said.

William thought it best to leave it at that for now and return to Toulouse to collect a hire van. He left the Mercedes there and drove the van the long way round to home.

"All on course, Arthur?" William asked when he arrived.

"Yes. We can load up tonight, do the hippy collections in the morning, and then deliver mid-day on the plateau."

Chapter 19

All went as normal. They pulled up, van first, then motorbike. There were greeted by a smiling Adrian, who exchanged cash for bags.

"Thanks, boys. Perfect and on time, as usual. By the way, they say it's very good quality. Also, my younger brother is keen to be trained up, ready to take a load off your shoulders in future."

"I know he is your brother," William said, "but I have to ask. Is he one hundred per cent trustworthy?"

"Yes, I guarantee it," Adrian responded confidently. "I am sure he is the perfect person for us all. Let's face it, he would have to be, or all of us would be fucked. You will like him. He is very respectful and will start as soon as you like. He has a lady friend with her own house fairly close to you, and she will know nothing."

"Okay, let us meet him this week. Ring me and arrange a meeting. We need to get back now."

They were soon home with the cash hidden away as usual.

William needed to get back to Toulouse to hand the van in and on to Limoges with the old Mercedes to do some more mock menacing. He was not to know, but they had already spotted him and were busy plotting his demise. William did have a strong feeling he had been made. Warning bells were ringing, and from now on, everything he did would be on the assumption he was being carefully watched. He drove quickly through Limoges, changing course enough to throw anyone off the scent, then parked for the night. He got into his sleeping bag. He was going to go for breakfast in Limoges at the same cafe every day. They must be sure now this was his area. He had now noticed all three watching him. He was sure they would have taken photos and sent them back for confirmation.

It was now time again to make a delivery with Arthur. He left the Mercedes and slipped off at night. He collected the hire van he had ordered, and again, driving the long way round, William made his way back to Arthur and loaded up.

The following morning, they were up early to collect from the hippies, ready to meet with Adrian. When they arrived, his younger brother Arneux was with him.

"Arny for short," he said. "If you like, we will follow you back now."

"Sure, let's get started and keep it in the family," William said.

They drove back and showed Arny to his room. "Tomorrow, Arthur will start your training, and there is no one better. One golden rule: say nothing to anyone under any circumstances ... Never bring anyone here, understood?"

"Yes, Adrian already told me the rules. I am very grateful for the chance."

"Well, Arthur," William said as he was getting ready to set off. "He should be a great help to you, and I think I will have sorted out my problems in the next couple of weeks."

They hugged one another.

"Be careful, William. Please be careful."

"Don't worry; I will."

He drove off, and as he got to Toulouse, he noticed Julian and his machine. He was obviously just finishing for the day. His wife was there with his car, picking him up. William stopped for a chat.

"Hi, Julian. You are a long way from home."

"Yes, I am very busy, but I don't like turning anything down. This is a job for Toulouse Council, and they pay well, so no messing about – I work late if necessary. What brings you out this way?" he asked.

"I am still trying to tie up loose ends," William replied. "So, for now, I am living out this way while I am being watched. It keeps them away from my real area. I have got an old Mercedes I use here, and I would never be surprised if it came to grief, them hoping I am in it. I might need to be yet. We will see."

"I know you don't need to be told to be careful, but what I would like to say is if there is anything I can do to help, and I mean anything, just say. I guarantee to be your man."

"Thanks, Julian. Somehow I think I already knew that, but I will try not to ask too much – if anything. Good luck."

"Good luck to you, too, Boss."

William turned, waved to Julian's wife and left. He returned the hire van and made his way back under cover of darkness to his old car, should he trust it. He quickly checked underneath with his torch and the wiring under the bonnet. There was nothing obvious. He came to the conclusion that, in fact, the most likely thing was that they would probably put a tracker on it and then corner him somewhere. He would take a chance tonight. That also would mean that he had no idea they had him in their sights so they could choose the best time to strike. The one thing he did know was if, as he thought, they had a tracker on his car, then he could choose a place, park, get ready and wait.

The next morning, he drove to see Julian. "Have you any explosives on you, Julian?"

"Yes, the usual stuff for stumps."

"I need some today."

"It is in the van in a strong box. Help yourself."

"Thanks."

William drove to a lonely spot by a ravine, parked near the edge and waited. Half an hour later, they arrived, cautiously driving to within four or five metres. His engine was running.

"It's now or never," he said to himself.

William accelerated hard and rammed into the side of them. They were not expecting it. He backed off a bit and rammed again and again. All four doors were now jammed tight shut. Twice more, and he had pushed it and them over the edge. It smashed loudly down. He took out his wallet and personal possessions. He threw them, along with some of his clothes, into his car, checked where the car below was and aimed his to go over and land on it, or close enough. He put it in gear and jumped out to watch it go over the edge. Standing back, both cars were now on fire then there was an almighty bang. The explosives finished off all people and both cars. Nothing survived, and nothing was left to be recognised. He quickly left the scene, walking through the trees and fields towards Julian.

By the time he reached him, the flashing lights and sirens of police cars seemed to be everywhere.

"Julian, put me in the digger bucket and lift me up out of sight. If anyone asks, and I hope they do, you saw a black car chasing a red car. He was trying to ram it, and it sounded as though he managed it in the end."

The police did arrive, talked to Julian, and he helpfully obliged. The local news reporter did the same. By the end of the day, the papers and television news was full of how the red and black cars were jousting, but as the red car forced the black over the edge, it lost control and ended over as well, landing on top. One must have had explosives in, so no one survived.

Julian lowered the bucket and William, saying, "It looks like it worked, Boss. Nothing left to be recognised. My wife will be here soon. She will take us back to the yard. I didn't tell her to come earlier; I thought it best to leave everything as normal as possible."

"Perfect, Julian. Exactly what was needed, but I could do with a coat or blanket. I was freezing in an iron bucket in my underwear."

"Here, have my coat. We don't want to shock the wife now, do we? And by the way, she is good. She won't ask a thing. She might wonder, but she won't ask."

"The perfect woman then," William said, and they both laughed.

She arrived, looked a bit surprised but accepted it all as Julian had said she would. She drove them into the yard.

As William got out of the van, revealing his bare legs, Tom joked, "What have you two been up to with poor William? Actually, no, don't tell me! Nothing surprises me anymore, particularly here at work!"

Arthur came out of the house. "Are you okay, William?"

"Yes, all finished. That's the good news. The bad news is I lost a good pair of jeans, a jumper and a watch!!" He turned to Tom and Julian. "Thanks, boys. I owe you!"

"You owe us nothing! Well, perhaps breakfast in the morning."

"Breakfast it is then, with pleasure."

He went inside with Arthur. "It will be on the news in the morning."

"That good was it then?"

"Yes, it went with a bang, you might say, and all because I guessed they had put a tracker on my car. From then on, I knew I could have the upper hand and choose where and when to suit me. Let's watch the news and have a beer. I need an early night. My nerves are shot, and so am I."

"Bullshit, William. I don't believe you have nerves, just big bollocks, ha ha ha."

It was on the news – a short version – but by morning, it would be the long, proper story.

"How is work, Arthur, and our new apprentice?" William asked.

"He is a quick learner, and I think he is the right type, but time will tell. We will be with him most of the time, so we will see, and Adrian swears by him. Family loyalty counts for a lot. He goes to the girlfriend quite a bit. He told her he is in sales, working for a company buying and selling from China. I did check her out from a distance. She is a real looker and seems straight enough. I'm completely happy with him, so all good – for now, anyway."

"One more delivery, and it will be time for the girls to go to Spain for the final signings. I will talk to the bank in the morning to arrange for the garage money to be paid to the lawyer, ready for the big day, but now first things first. Breakfast with the boys, as I promised, then a hard day's harvesting. It should be easier now there are three of us, and it's another learning curve for Arny."

Chapter 20

In the morning, it was bacon sandwiches and coffee for all in the yard. Arthur called it 'the exotic oil drum breakfast' as the tables and seats were inevitably oil drums. Somehow, it made it better and more authentic.

"Thanks, Boss, just what the doctor ordered," Tom said. "By the way, did you see the news this morning?"

"No, not yet, but we will soon. There is always something new on the news," William said, chuckling. Of course, they had seen it but were happy to leave it at that.

Harvest started. Arny was pulling his weight but needed to be shown how to trim enough but not too much. As in most jobs, it is an acquired art. Everything had its first trim and was hung in the drying room for a week. This was the really smelly stage, but they had a strong extraction fan blowing it up the chimney high into the air, well above nosey noses. The next task and lesson was learning how to take hundreds of cuttings from the big mother plants and get them rooting strong enough to put them on the first stage of the conveyor system. All stages needed different strength nutrients and length of exposure time under grow lights. Arny had his regular jobs, checking the pH of the water and then the water levels in the tanks. He kept the place clean and dropped all old plants and trimmings into the trailer below the window. There were a lot of necessary but mundane jobs to be done that the boys were happy not to do any more but which Arny really enjoyed.

William phoned Jane and sang, "Happy days are here again ... Hi, Jane."

"Thank god, William. I am so relieved!"

"Two weeks at the most, Jane, and you will need to be in Spain with Angelina. Then you will be busy. Lots to do before the grand opening."

"Hard work. Do I care? No! I love the idea, and Angelina does too. Neither of us can wait."

"I spoke to the lawyer in Spain. He has received the money, ready to pay on the day. Meanwhile, sweetheart, you need to enjoy Paris as much as possible now because you might not get there again for a while. I will call you later in the week. Start packing. We will hire a truck and collect you both. Bye for now."

Arthur added, "I will talk to Angelina tonight. It will give them chance to think of any questions they need answering. No doubt there will be plenty, and you know how it is – the moment you put the phone down, you think of things you should have said or asked."

"Let us go into town tonight for a beer. We ought to be seen around as though nothing has happened," William said.

"Yes, I agree, although they won't have expected us since Jane left."

"No, but they will probably be asking when she will be coming back to work next summer. Well, we know the answer to that one, don't we? But I suppose we say nothing."

"Yes, best to know nothing in as many places and as often as possible. Nothing is best. Something means questions."

"Nothing it is, then."

"It's a strange feeling, being sat here without a care, isn't it?" Arthur said.

"It certainly is, and soon we will no longer need to come here. I don't think we will need it or miss it. It has played its part. Mainly, it provided us with the ladies that were absolutely right for us."

"Yes, so thank you, town," Arthur said.

"I am looking forward to tomorrow. We have not had breakfast and casually worked at home for ages. When we next go to Andorra, I need a watch, and I must arrange a Spanish bank account. We need to make a list of things we need to do in the nearest town to the hotel. This coming weekend, when we deliver, I think we should go straight over Andorra into Spain for the day, do some of these jobs and come back. After all, we have our apprentice to look after everything without us. Let's make use of him."

"And we should check out the whole area and also find a decorator. So that's a plan, then."

The rest of the week was spent working and teaching Arny. By Sunday, they were ready to deliver. They had the van loaded and left Arny with his instructions. After an hour, they had collected from the hippies and were well on the way to Adrian. They were earlier than usual, but he was already waiting.

"Arny seems to have been a good choice and is learning fast," William said. "We are on our way to Spain to look at some property. We will call on you on the way back as we need to do some shopping."

They drove straight to the Costa Brava and the hotel. They both liked it even more this time. They went with the agent to pay for the insurance and then visited a bank. They both opened accounts and arranged a safe locker each to put the cash they had with them in, keeping some back for shopping. They needed to do it because carrying money over the border could be a problem if they were stopped. They found a decorator and got some rough prices. They circled the area and agreed this was a good place to live and for business. They sampled the restaurants before heading for Andorra. They did their shopping, including buying a watch. They also timed their journey as, for a while anyway, they would be driving back to work at least once a month to keep an eye on things and do deliveries. It didn't seem too bad, and they would enjoy a trip to or through Andorra from the other side for a change, as would the girls for shopping.

They spent a couple of hours with Adrian before the final leg back, dropping the van off on the way. The two tired men were soon in bed.

Early risers, they were soon checking the grow rooms the following morning. Arny had been to work already, and it was all nicely under control.

Arthur rang Angelina. "Hi, Angie. Have you packed?"

"Nearly, just a few things."

"What size van do we need, do you think, for you both?"

"Something like a large transit, as Jane has a few things in her old apartment she would like to get on the way back," Angelina answered.

"That's good. We will arrive early Saturday morning to collect you both. We'll bring you here first; then we will take the car as well to our new home. It will mean more room, and we will want the car there, too. Have you chosen a new name yet?"

"No, but we are both leaning towards Angels, so I expect that is what it will be."

"Well, my love, we spoke to the lawyer and agent and insured it. On Saturday, we will collect you both and come here before heading off early Sunday morning for Spain. We will stay in a rival hotel on Sunday night close by as we have the final signing at 9 am on Monday, so a big weekend and a bigger Monday. There is a lot of bedding and a washing machine, in case! Also, there is a list of numbers like laundry, etc. Knowing you, even if it looks clean, you will want to wash some before we sleep there. Am I right, or am I right?"

"You are right. Luckily, we have everything, including washing powder. We should have all we need when we arrive."

"Right, sweetheart. We will see you on Saturday morning. I will drive as I know the way, having been there before, and he needs a break."

The week went fast. They harvested and hung to dry, ready to deliver the week after. On Friday, they hired a larger van than asked for, to be on the safe side, and hit the road for Paris. They would be early and knew they would be welcome to stay the night and be on the way back Saturday morning, getting home before dark. They were all glad to be ahead of schedule and could leave after breakfast in the morning and take their time.

"We will take a table and chairs into the garden for breakfast," Arthur suggested, thinking the girls might not like the usual oil drum breakfast. They wasted no time eating and drinking a quick coffee; they were just longing to get to see their new home again. The two vehicles travelled in tandem, mainly so they would stop for refreshments and lunch together.

They finally pulled into the hotel's ample car park. They would leave the vehicles there, ready for the morning. They found rooms close by and booked in. The agent's and lawyer's offices were close by, so there was no hurry. They all went for an early night.

Chapter 21

It was two very excited girls at breakfast the next morning. It took nearly two hours before all the formalities were completed. Then the boys took the girls to the bank and opened an account with cash in the girls' names and with the business name, "Angels." They would get their cards and chequebooks at the end of the week. Until then, they would use cash which, of course, the boys had in the bank's private safes, ready and waiting.

"Now, let's get back to our hotel," Arthur said. "William and I will unload the van, and you two go to the list of contacts to call the cleaners. Make a list of alterations and decorations that are needed, then ring the decorators. We should get organised and comfortable today. There is no hurry, but in a few days, we will have to go back to work and return the van. We will need to go back quite often for a while – at least once a month – mixing that with shopping in Andorra."

The girls worked hard and eagerly on their new project, loving every moment of it. They designed the new Angels sign, the kitchen was ready, and they had hired a cook. Initially, they would open with minimal staff to check business possibilities first. They were continually interviewing potential staff. They had a nice roomy office with two large desks. The organising and advertising would be important, and somewhere comfortable to do it from was crucial. They were even starting to work out budgets and sensible costings using the few examples they had. The most impressive thing was just how alike these girls were and how well they got on. Long may it continue. The two men had been solid for years, which ensured their success, and now the girls were the same.

"Well, girls, if you need advice, both Arthur and myself will try to help, but as much as possible, we would like you two to make all the decisions. Firstly, because it is your business, and secondly, the best way to learn is to try on your own. You will probably make mistakes, but I doubt you will make the same mistake twice. Nothing ventured, nothing gained, remember? So have a go; I am sure you will succeed. Two more days and we will have to leave you to it. We need to take the van back and do some work. We will be back in a week at the most. We will leave the car here for you. The keys are on the hook in the office. You both drive, don't you?" William asked.

"Yes, but we'll probably be too busy here for a week or two," Jane said. It will be good to have it – just in case. The decorator is coming tomorrow. You will see him for a day or two just to make sure he knows the score. Some men just don't listen to women. It's best he knows there is a man around."

In fact, he was there first thing with his partner and materials ready to go.

Arthur gave them their instructions but added, "The women are the bosses, and they have the final say. We are going to be away for a few days, but the girls will be in touch with us daily."

Once told the scheme, they just got on without question.

"Bye for now. We will be back soon. Don't work too hard, girls."

They left to drive straight home in time to help Arny finish preparing for delivery. There were a few things to sort out with Arny, but mostly he had learned and not forgotten, meaning they were all happy and loaded for delivery. They helped Arny reorganise the beds with new plants. The next week would just be checking levels and lights before the busy harvesting of the following week.

Morning came, and they were both keen to get going. They were loaded, and Arthur was on the motorbike, ready to play the trail finder: to be five minutes in front checking for possible police. They headed for the hippy camps to collect from the grateful hippies who had by now come to rely on the cash for their keep and worked hard to please.

"Soon, they were on the plateau with Adrian.

"It's all about the same, Adrian. All okay here?" William asked.

"Yes, all smooth."

"We need to get back today. We are looking at some cheap diesel vans. We need one and don't want to keep hiring." The truth was they needed a van or people carrier to collect provisions and items for the hotel and as a general runabout when the car was not available: a vehicle that the boys could use for deliveries if needed. They eventually found one that the girls would be happy driving. They made an offer, and it was accepted.

They then returned the hired one and took the motorbike back home safely into its shed. They would stay most of the morning with Arny. They agreed to a good wage for him with the advice, "Don't be a spender. For one, it attracts unwanted attention. And two, you might want to buy into the business at some point, and you would need cash for that."

"Yes, sure, I will be careful."

"We are going back to Paris at midday," William lied. "Any problems, call us."

"Yes, I will, but I have got the hang of most things now."

"Right, we will be off, then. It's an hour or so longer in this van than a car, but we needed one, and it is cheap transport."

They were soon in Andorra doing some shopping. They bought Baileys and spirits for the hotel bar, along with treats for the girls.

"When shall we move the cash from the house?" Arthur asked. "Should we move it to Spain and feed some gradually into the bank or put it in the bank lockers?"

"Well, normally, I would put it in the bank, but I just don't trust Spanish banks."

"That's a decision for another day then, William. Let's get back to the girls as soon as possible."

They parked the hotel van next to their car and looked at the freshly painted facade of the hotel. It certainly looked different now that the Angels sign was in place.

"If the inside is half as good as the outside, I will be very pleased. What do you think?" Arthur asked William.

"I think the girls have been jolly good organisers, which is a relief. Bodes well for the future."

They had been spotted, and two elegant ladies were coming down the steps smiling.

"Do you two men want to book a room? We do have a couple available," Angelina said.

Arthur was quick with a reply. "This place looks a bit too posh for us. I doubt we can afford it."

"No, Arthur," William added, "we need something cheaper with a horny landlady or two."

"You can come in, but you will have to earn your keep. Are you happy to try?"

"We will try and be judged by you two professional ladies."

"Stop loitering! Get in now. We need you, and you can look at what we have done inside. It's nearly all finished and within budget. We still need some curtains and carpets, but everything else is done."

"Well, as soon as you like, you can go shopping. We bought that van for that type of stuff. It holds a lot and drives really nicely. I know it's a van, but I think you will like it. It's got windows all around, so it's easy to see out to drive and small enough to reverse into anywhere."

They walked inside. "Wow, it looks great!" William said. "Where is the honeymoon suite?"

"That's for newlyweds, and I don't know any of those, do you?" Jane asked, hinting broadly.

William looked at Arthur, then at the floor, and then tried to talk, but it was awkward.

Angelina helped the situation. "We have food. Let's eat and have an early night. Welcome home, boys."

"I must use the loo. Which is the nearest one?"

"The one along the corridor from the dining room"

On the way back, William passed Arthur, who answered the unspoken question.

"Why not? I would like it. What about you?"

"Yes, I would. It feels right, but I didn't know how you felt after your first wife," William said.

"I loved her intensely, but she is gone and has been for at least ten years now. I need to move on."

"As long as you are sure, Arthur. We have been pals for so long now, in fact, ever since my divorce. I couldn't do it on my own, but together, I would love to."

"Same for me, William."

"What, now? A joint proposal?"

"What? Kneeling together?"

They both laughed. "First, let's eat."

This simple situation was, in fact, a first. These two ladies had made a meal for their men together in their home. Since they met quite a few years earlier, neither of these men had had a lady friend provide for and feed them. Now, in one go, they both had. William dropped something on the floor. Both men got down to look for it. It was a minute or so before Jane first, and then Angelina realised. William was kneeling at Jane's feet, and Arthur was kneeling at hers when in unison, they said, "Will you marry us?"

Then, William, alone, said, "Marry me, please, Jane."

Then Arthur added, "Marry me, Angelina."

"Well, we know you boys do everything together, but I never imagined this one. But we will, won't we, Angelina?"

They had spent all week talking about the possibility, so they both knew the other's feelings. "Let's set a date tomorrow – when we have time to think," Angelina said. "All four of us are planners and would like a say. You boys, possibly for the gimmick, proposed together, but I know I speak for Jane as well: we insist we have a double wedding, please."

Chapter 22

Although the beds were perfect and the company better, this four were always up early for breakfast together. They sat around joking casually; this was the highlight of the day.

"What is the plan for your day, girls?" Arthur asked.

"It's carpet and curtain day; ready for our grand opening this weekend," Angelina said.

"Do you need us?"

"No, Jane and me will manage. We will take the van, although we will probably get everything delivered. We already looked, so we are almost sure what we will get, but we will enjoy another drive around to see what is new."

"Yes, but we will be back for lunch," Jane said, "What are you boys doing?"

"We are going to have a walk on the front. It's a chance to unwind and meet a few locals, perhaps."

"I will enjoy that, William. When did we ever walk anywhere?"

"Never, let's do it."

They left the room cleaner in charge.

"This is the life, William," Arthur said.

"It is, but tomorrow we swim while it is warm enough. Are you game?"

"Yes. I am sure we are going to be furniture movers and curtain fitters this afternoon for the girls."

Of course, they both acted as though this was a hardship, but really, they both quite enjoyed the involvement, helping their ladies achieve what was turning out to be a great project.

As they walked into the car park, they could see the girls with their van and another larger furniture van parked alongside. "It looks as though they have had a successful morning," Arthur said.

"Yes, I am beginning to hope the spending is finished, and now the organising of the opening can officially start the business." William addressed Jane and Angelina. "Have you managed to get everything to finish this job, girls?"

"Yes, that's it. A day of fitting, and we can open. Thanks for being patient with us, William."

"We all need this to be right, and you have completed it as we wanted, haven't they, Arthur?"

"Yes, thanks, girls. It's looking great now it is finished."

"Let us arrange the wedding as soon as possible," Angelina said.

"What about guests?" Arthur asked. "I just realised none of us has relations."

"All we need are witnesses," William replied. "Jane and I will be yours, and Angelina and you will be ours. Now that is sorted, when and where? For me, it's here and in two weeks' time. We are due back in France soon for three days. Then when we are back, we have the wedding, which gives us two weeks before the grand opening: time for a honeymoon. That all fits. Well, how about you girls?"

"That's perfect, William," Jane said. "We had better see the local priest, or whatever they call him here, and make sure it is possible. That's our job for tomorrow."

Everything had gone easily up to that point, but after talking to the priest, they found it very complicated to get married there, even with their passports and willingness to donate to the church. They sat in town with a coffee, feeling deflated and looking over the harbour where a large cruise ship was just leaving. Despite the setback, William was deep in thought. Perhaps a cruise honeymoon trip was due anyway.

"You three stay here a minute. I have an idea. I won't be long, okay?" he said as he got up to leave.

"Alright. We are in no hurry to go anywhere now."

William had noticed a large travel agency two roads along. He walked in and sat down at one of the desks. "Can you give me details of cruises?"

"Certainly, sir. We have one leaving every week, taking in Portofino, Capri, Venice and Pompeii."

"Perfect. When is the next one?"

"One just left, so the next is one week and a day from today. It comes back in a week, then takes a full day to be thoroughly cleaned and restocked, ready to go again."

"That is perfect. As long as I can book two of the best cabins for honeymoons."

"Yes, sir. They are much more expensive, so they are often available."

"Right. Book them in my name. I will give you a large cash deposit now and the rest in cash in the next three days."

"Thank you, sir. Any deposit will do."

"One more question. I have heard that a sea captain can legally perform a wedding ceremony. Can your captain?"

"Yes, sir. This does happen from time to time."

"Can you tell me what we will need?"

"Passports and proof you are single, and as many personal documents as possible for identity. Do you want me to warn the captain in advance to make sure everything is in order?"

"Yes, please. I will leave my details and contact numbers. We live in the town at the Angels hotel."

"Wow! That has been transformed. It looks lovely now. I have seen the two ladies walking round the town always looking happy."

"They are angels. I am marrying one, and my best pal is marrying the other one, hopefully now on your cruise ship."

"That is so romantic. I'll hardly be able to contain myself when they walk past in future."

"Please try because we want it to be a surprise. We found out today that it is complicated to get married here and would take months. This will be a great surprise. We would like to keep it secret as long as possible."

"My advice to you then, sir, is that we arrange with the captain that the marriage takes place on the second day. That way, you will be outside the three-mile limit, and it is when the boat runs close to the isle of Capri or a point of your choice. Also, you will be married soon enough to enjoy most of the trip as honeymooners."

"Yes, please do that. You should have been a wedding planner."

"My pleasure, sir."

He was soon back with the others. "What have you been up to, William?" Jane asked.

"I have been selfish."

"How?" she asked, and the others waited.

"Well, you see that cruise ship just disappearing? It is going to Portofino, Capri, Rome and Venice. Where else ...? Ah, I remember – Pompeii. One week and two days from now, we will be on it to at least have our honeymoon before Angels is open for business."

"That is not selfish, William."

"It was, because I should have checked with you all first before booking it,"

"You have already booked?"

"Yes, is that alright?"

"Of course it is. We needed a boost after the wedding problems. Another hour or so of people-watching, and we should get back to Angels. I like it there," Arthur joked.

"So do I. There is no place like home," William said.

"Yes," agreed Jane. "So nice to hear it. Tonight, I fancy a liqueur and some nice music before an early night. You boys are off again tomorrow. Can you get an assortment of liqueurs from Andorra on the way back? If we make sure our standard of food is good, attracting the right customers, I think they would appreciate a good selection to round the evening off."

"Let us get back to try what we have while testing our sound system. I don't even know what CDs or programs are available. We can use Bluetooth, but a nice selection of our own would be best."

"Let us test everything; then what we need, we can get in Andorra on the way back, but as far as music is concerned, I think you girls should find and buy locally."

No sooner were they home than the liqueurs came under scrutiny. "Some of these are really nice, but once your pallet is accustomed to one taste, it is difficult to try another," Jane said. "This tasting is going to take some time."

They all laughed.

"I think we should just buy a few on the way back and make sure we have whatever is asked for," William said.

It was bedtime, and the girls, in particular, were feeling a bit heady from the alcohol. As the boys would be leaving in the morning, all four of them wanted reasonably clear heads. They all had unspoken plans which had been passing through their minds for some time. And now, they were all about to come to fruition.

The next morning William and Arthur were soon on their way in the van again over the Pyrenees back to work and Arny. On the way, William busily explained the plan to get married on the cruise.

"What do you think, Arthur?"

"What do I think? What do I think? Pure genius! That's what I think. It will blow the girls' minds! Well done, pal. I cannot wait. WOW!"

"Glad you agree, Arthur. I have struggled to keep quiet, but I'm glad you know now!"

"Thank god you did not tell me while we were there yesterday. I would have been like a dog with two cocks. How did you manage to keep quiet?"

"With great difficulty, pal. With very great difficulty."

They drove into the yard and chatted with Tom, who was busy as usual. "Have you seen much of our housesitter, Arny?"

"No, not a lot. He is friendly enough but keeps himself to himself, never has visitors and goes out most days for a while."

"Tom, I need you to make us a lockable box that I can carry tools in for the van," William said.

"When do you want it?"

"The day after tomorrow, if possible."

"What about one like the one Julian keeps his explosives in? Only they sell those as strong boxes in the hardware store with padlocks. They cost around fifty euros."

"Yes, that will do. Plenty big enough. But also, I would like a wooden panel that could be put in the bottom as a partition or false floor."

"I will cut one out of a board as soon as I know the size."

"I will get one later, Tom, and leave it here for you to measure,"

"Sure, leave it to me."

William joined Arthur inside with Arny bagging up the next delivery. "It's just about the same amount as last time. It will keep Adrian happy."

'Yes,' thought Arthur, 'plus the other lots we pick up on the way from the hippies. Adrian should be very happy.'

They were loaded by the evening. William had bought his strong box and left it with Tom to make the floor. The evening was spent moving pots and plants around and loading up all stage beds to the maximum, as usual.

"Any questions, Arny?"

"No, all good. Adrian pays my money straight into my bank in Andorra. I have my cards that I can draw cash from the hole in the wall whenever I need some. We still have enough nutrients and bulbs in stock for possibly six months or more. It would be nice to have a cash box to buy sundry bits and pieces for breakages and new compost."

Arthur pulled a small roll of notes from his pocket and handed it to him. "Buy a cash box and put this in Arny. I wish you had mentioned it before. It was something we had not thought of."

"That's alright. I have not needed much so far. It's nice to know it's there now – just in case."

"Let's get some sleep. We have a big day tomorrow."

Chapter 23

They were up and away early, collected from the hippies, and then delivered to Adrian. He was his usual, happy self.

"Thank you, boys."

"We have some shopping to do in Andorra tomorrow. We will call in and see you there. Can you sort out half a dozen bottles of good liqueurs for us to buy? The next trip, it will need to be good wines."

They drove from there to town and to the lawyer's office.

"We need to make our wills. Will it take long?"

"That all depends on how complicated it is," the lawyer replied.

"We'll both make basic wills for the moment. We can get more involved another day when we have discussed it more, but right now, we have our passports with us. We both have bank accounts and lock boxes in three banks: one here, one in

Spain and one each in the UK. Also, we have a house just outside the village – half each. If anything happens to me, my half goes to Arthur. As for the money and belongings in the banks, everything from me goes to Jane, who will be my wife in one week."

"And all mine," Arthur said, "goes to Angelina, who will also be my wife in a week."

"Well, that is straightforward enough. I will get something drawn up for you tomorrow. Is that alright and soon enough?"

"Perfect, thank you."

"I just need an address and contact number for the ladies," the lawyer added.

"That's easy. They both live at the same address, and I have their phone and email addresses with me," William replied.

"Right. I'll see you tomorrow, then."

"Thank you. We do a lot of travelling and one on a cruise soon. I suddenly thought we should do this to save any trouble. If you tell us how much, I will pay you in cash tomorrow – if that suits you."

"Yes, thank you. Come by any time after 1 pm."

They went back to the yard. Tom had finished putting the false floor in the toolbox, and Julian was sitting on it. Both were waiting to see them. "William, fetch some beers from the house," Arthur said. "Let us have a drink with our mates."

William quickly returned with four bottles. "It's good to see both of you together and give you our news. We are both getting married in a week's time and going on a cruise for our honeymoon."

"Congratulations, both of you," Tom said. "We wish you the best of luck. We are very happy for you, aren't we, Julian?"

"Certainly, and if you get a chance for us all to be here together again, it would be special to have a party like we had last time. Our wives have not stopped talking about it."

"We will do our best. We would love to do it all again. Anyway, how is business for you two? Plenty of groundwork, Julian?"

"Yes, it's been really good, and having a yard we don't have to pay for makes so much more possible, doesn't it, Tom?"

"It certainly does. We can't thank you enough."

"Stay happy and friendly. You owe us nothing. If you ever have a problem or need anything, ring us, please. We are off to Andorra to do some shopping tomorrow, so we won't see you for two or three weeks."

They finished the beers and went in to see Arny, leaving Tom and Julian to finish up and go home.

Arny was about to go to see his girlfriend but had waited to talk to William. "There is a lot of plant rubbish in the pit, and some smells a bit. Could someone cover it with dirt? I emptied the trailer again today."

"Okay, I will see to it. Goodnight. See you in the morning."

Arny left, and William quickly went out and caught Julian. "Julian, as soon as possible, can you put a bucket of dirt on the rubbish in the pit? Just enough to cover the garden waste."

"Sure. I'll do it first thing in the morning on my way out," Julian replied.

"Thanks, Julian." William picked up the tool-box, carried it into the kitchen and lifted the false floor. "I think we have to take a chance, Arthur and move a lot of the cash now – it needs to go to Spain. If there was ever trouble here, the place would be searched from one end to the other, and they would find everything. But if we do, we won't be able to take much alcohol."

"Some of the alcohol can wait," Arthur said. "Four bottles between us will be enough for now."

William agreed. "Yes, we can get the rest of the alcohol any time. Then, of course, one other important thing: two wedding rings!!"

"Jesus, William! I had not given that a thought. What a cock up that would have been!"

"Well, right now, Arthur, let's put the cash in the toolbox under the false floor and then put in a good selection of tools and snow chains. We will need them in the winter to get over the mountain."

They filled the box and, between them, put it in the van. "We will buy the chains in Andorra; they are cheaper there," William said.

Arny came back in good time and had coffee with them before checking the nutrients.

"Arny, we might not be back for three weeks as we are having a holiday, but carry on as usual, and we will deliver then."

One pm came, and they returned to the lawyers. They signed, paid and collected copies of their wills and were very quickly on the way over the border into Andorra, not stopping until they were outside Adrian's shop.

"We will pay you for all the liqueurs now, but only take four bottles with us, if that's okay?"

"Yes, all good. I do understand – there are all sorts of reasons to be careful – some more important than others."

"Yes, it's only today when it might be a problem. In the meantime, who do you recommend we go to to buy wedding rings?"

"There are two friends of mine with shops who will give you a good deal."

"We will go now."

Adrian pointed out the shops.

They entered and went to speak to the owner.

"Yes, Adrian rang me. He said you wanted classy but not silly prices. What did you have in mind?"

"Two white gold mix wedding rings, both y7 in size," William said.

"I can show you several, but the two I like the most are identical, so we would need to stamp a different message inside each one. These are the ones. What do you think?"

"Well, I like them a lot. How about you, Arthur?"

"Very nice. It's roughly what I hoped for."

"We will take them. Can you put the message inside now?"

They chose a message each and kept it secret. When they were ready, the rings were put in their boxes; one marked J and the other A. They paid, thanked the man and left. They bought their washing powder and snow chains, putting the chains in the toolbox. They put the liqueurs and washing powder in a cardboard box.

"Time to go, Arthur. We don't want to be back too late."

"No, let's go, William, and hope we don't get stopped and searched."

"Think positive, Arthur, and we will be okay."

"I believe you."

At the border, they were stopped and questioned by the *Douane*. The toolbox was opened, and the cardboard box searched."

"You are half a bottle of alcohol over," the officer said.

"We can't be. We only have two bottles each. We were trying to make sure we were under."

"You made a mistake. These bottles are litre bottles – they are slightly larger."

"What do we do? We brought them for our lady friends. Do we lose one, or do we pay the extra tax? What usually happens?"

"Have you not been stopped before?"

"No."

"Well, I see you have brought them chocolates."

"Yes, they deserve a treat."

"Okay, but what is the washing powder for? Another treat?"

They all laughed.

"Right, you two," the officer said. "You go and treat your ladies."

"Thank you. See you in a few weeks. We work in France once or twice a month."

"Safe trip."

They got back in the van and drove home.

"Four bottles was a lucky choice, Arthur."

"It certainly was," he replied.

The rest of the journey was uneventful. They were soon home. The name, 'home,' had a wonderful ring to it when Jane and Angelina were there waiting. They went in carrying the chocolates and alcohol along with the washing powder.

"Angelina will have the alcohol; I will have the chocolates," Jane said.

"Oh no, we will share the chocolate," Angelina said. "I am seeing you with different eyes, Jane. Hand over the chocolates now!" They were both laughing and having a half-hearted struggle which ended with the tin falling open between them. These two had the type of relationship that always ended with a lot of laughing.

"Do not eat the mauve ones, Angelina, or there will be trouble."

"You, Jane, are a chocoholic!"

"You, too, Angelina."

"We are so alike."

"I know," Jane said. "I sometimes wonder how on earth we got together. Also, William and Arthur. I am sure we are closer than sisters. Much closer. The four of us must have been meant for one another. It's a great feeling."

"Yes, but you still are not having the chocs!!"

"Alright, we'll share, then."

"Goodnight, Jane."

"Goodnight, Angelina. See you in the morning."

Chapter 24

It was very special for the four of them to be back together. They were up early, not just looking forward to breakfast but the chats and friendships more so.

Jane opened with a joke. "I forgot to put the chocolates in the safe last night."

"Good morning, everyone. Coffee is on. Who wants a cooked breakfast?" Angelina asked.

"Not for us. It looks like toast all round. What are our plans for today?" William asked.

"I think we need to pack for the trip. It's close now, and they do have posh dances. We must take special dresses, and you boys will need a suit. You had better go to get suits this morning."

"Yes, straight after breakfast. William, okay with you?" Arthur asked.

This was not one of their favourite jobs. Clothes buying normally meant just jeans and a top, but the secret part of this trip made it much more important than that. They would have to grit their teeth and complete the mission to buy suits, shirts and ties, plus of course, the always-needed socks and underwear.

With the bags of their purchases in hand, they returned proudly for the girls to check over, approve and pack. They were only too pleased to hand everything over as packing was another much-hated job. Luckily for them, the ladies enjoyed it.

Angelina inspected the purchases. "I cannot wait to see you two suited and booted in these!"

"Do any of us need anything else, or can we close the cases?" William asked.

"They are done and checked, so close them and leave them in the hall," Jane replied.

It barely felt like a day had gone when they called a taxi to take them and the cases to the boat.

"Do not forget your passports. I have got the tickets and paperwork," William said. "We are ready to go."

First, they went to the ticket office. They were checked in, and their cases were taken from them.

"They will be in your cabins, waiting," the member of staff said. "Here are your keys. You will be shown to your cabins as you board. Have a good trip."

Sure enough, they were shown all the way by a member of the crew. As they went, the other areas of the ship were pointed out. They were given a booklet with maps of the various floors shown. "This is a big ship. For the first few days, you could get lost, so keep a map with you," the crew member advised. "Here are your rooms. You are next-door neighbours, and the other side of these cabins is joined by a balcony and walkway with private seating areas."

He handed over the keys, and they eagerly entered.

"Enjoy. There is a phone inside. Should you need anything, call me."

These cabins had been expensive, but they could see why. They were far from ordinary.

"This is a dream, Arthur."

"Angelina, I am dreaming, too. Let us visit our neighbours before we unpack."

They knocked on William and Jane's door. A few seconds later, the door was opened, and a dishevelled couple appeared. They also had been impressed and started to get carried away. If Arthur had been a minute or so later, they would have been naked.

Arthur laughed. "So you love your room, too," he said, directing a wink at William.

"Well, it's all right," he said, winking back. "We were just unpacking."

"Yes, I see. Unpacking yourselves and not the suitcases."

All four were laughing.

"Angelina, I think we should do some unpacking, too, and leave them to finish theirs."

"Good idea, Arthur," she said. "See you two in an hour or two."

"Yes, but no rush!" William said.

Angelina and Arthur left, feeling in the mood for blatant pleasure.

A couple of hours later, both men were out on the balcony, looking at the sea. It would be a few hours yet before the boat could get underway.

"William, my man, this is already the best holiday I have ever had."

"Me too, Arthur, and it will get better. By tomorrow night, we will be married."

"Yes. Another amazing landmark!"

"Jane's asleep," William said.

"So is Angelina."

"Well, I have always said, if a job is worth doing, then do it properly. Be proud, Arthur, old friend. We can safely say we both did a very important job very properly and well."

They both laughed.

It was quite a while before the girls joined them. William said sarcastically, "Have you girls finished unpacking?"

"Not quite. I got side-tracked by a needy man," Angelina said.

Arthur chipped in. "And I got side-tracked by a greedy woman."

"Well, whoever was needy or greedy, no one was complaining," William said. "And the holiday has truly started with a bang."

"I am getting hungry," Jane said. "Shall we look for a snack somewhere? It is still too early for dinner."

"Let's go," William said. "I have a map. We don't need money; just charge anything to our room."

They had a snack and went back to their rooms. They had barely sat down before there was a knock at both doors.

"The captain would like you to join him at his table for dinner at eight or twenty hundred hours," a crew member announced.

"Tell him thank you," Angelina said. "We will be there!"

"Well, what about that?" William said. "First on the captain's table. I expect it is mainly the people on this deck – they are the most expensive cabins."

"Do we know what is for dinner yet?" Jane asked.

"No idea. There must be some sort of menu, but I am sure it will all be good!"

By evening they were ready and eager. As they approached the captain's table, he got up and came over. "You must be the two couples in the honeymoon suites," he said.

"Yes. We had a problem with getting married this week, but we will enjoy the holiday and sort it out as soon as possible afterwards."

"Well, that is sad, but please enjoy the trip. I am sure you will." He looked the boys squarely in the eyes, smiled and returned to his seat.

"Well done, Captain," William said quietly to Arthur.

"Yes," he replied.

The food was impressive. The cruise had been underway for around three hours now. The captain rose and went round the table, having a few words with everyone seated there. Eventually, he reached them.

"Thank you very much for being here to eat with me tonight. I would like to ask a favour of you four. Tomorrow, at twelve noon, could you be here wearing something special, as you did tonight, for photos? Then we will have lunch, leaving you plenty of time afterwards to change into casual clothes. We will be calling at Capri in the afternoon to stay the evening there."

Jane answered for all four of them. "Of course, Captain. We would love to, and thank you for keeping us informed."

"Twelve noon, then. I will look forward to it."

They went back to their rooms, ordered a nightcap liqueur and went to bed, tired. It had been a big day. Only the boys knew a bigger one was coming. They were all soon asleep.

They ordered both of the couple's breakfasts to be delivered to Jane and William's room.

"Looks like suits for lunch, William. They need breaking in," Arthur said.

"And you girls. Have you decided what you are going to wear?" William asked.

"I have. It has to be my best for the picture," Jane said.

"And me the same. And there is a hairdresser along the end."

"I know how particular you girls are. I will go and book you in for eleven o'clock. You do not need much, but we are on holiday." William was on the ball and trying to act casual.

"That is thoughtful, William," Jane said. "Thank you. You never cease to amaze me."

"Just trying to please. I will go along and book you in."

As he walked into the hairdresser's, the lady receptionist said, "We have been expecting you and guessed it would be 11 o'clock. Was I right?"

"You were. I am impressed. They will be here at 11 on the dot. Thank you."

He went back to the others. "That's arranged. Choose anything you like. They are prepared, and we are treating ourselves. We are on holiday!"

They went just before 11.

As they went, Arthur said, "Another half an hour, and we will start getting suited up. Let's sit on the balcony with a coffee for that half hour."

Well before twelve, they were locking their doors, all perfectly dressed and making the short walk to the main centre. They entered to the sound of the wedding march. The captain was standing under the floral wedding arch, and most of the people from the cabins on their deck were making an aisle.

Jane looked at William with a tear in her eye. "Us?" she said.

Arthur replied, "Yes. All four of us."

The girls carefully dabbed the little tears away without smudging their makeup. They walked slowly up the aisle. It was a dream. They walked without awareness of anything. The girls' minds were racing. The rings were placed on their fingers. They were married. Everyone was clapping and cheering.

William was the one with the words. He held up his hand, and the crowd quietened.

He made his speech, which started with, "Thank you so very much to you all. You have added that very important part to our wedding. This wedding means the world to us, and now, as I look around at all your happy faces, we will remember all of you and what you have contributed, along with our grandly official captain. Please join us for lunch and drinks. It will help complete this, our special day. Thank you."

It was lunchtime, and the boat had provided a special banquet in their honour.

Arthur whispered to William, "I will organise the champagne for everyone."

"Good idea, and you can thank them all personally as you do it. Just a word will mean a lot to them; they deserve it."

Arthur had the wine waiters and champagne trolley visiting all the tables. William had no idea what Arthur was saying, but they were all joking and laughing, obviously enjoying his attention. He was in his element.

"Look at your husband, Angelina. He is a star!"

"Yes, I know! How I am going to get over this, I do not know. What about you, Jane?"

"I am at a loss for words. I can feel a message in my ring. Have you got one? Mine says 'JANE, LOVE OF MY LIFE, WILLIAM' What did Arthur write, William?"

"I don't know; he never said."

Angelina answered. "You two are so alike. Mine, in small writing, says the same: 'To Angelina, love of my life, Arthur.' So, other than a different name, it's identical. Do either of you think differently? I doubt it – it's extraordinary."

Lunch was good, but the champagne, although excellent and appreciated, had slowed everyone down.

"Thank goodness they took the pictures first," Jane said.

The rest of the day was a blur. They did see some of Capri after docking, also managing to stretch their legs walking around. At the end of the day, they sat in silence on the balcony, looking over the sea and Capri.

"What a day, Arthur, what a day, Angelina, what a day Jane," William said.

"And also you, William. What a day," Jane said,

"We got married, Jane," Angelina said dreamily.

"I know, Angie. Amazing, isn't it?"

"It is now a proper honeymoon."

"Thank you, boys. It is time for bed, or we will fall asleep here," Jane said.

"Goodnight."

They all went to bed and slept late.

They eventually got up for breakfast. By then, the boat was on its way to Pompeii.

"This holiday is a lot harder than work," William commented.

"I am going to rest or sleep on the balcony until we dock in Pompeii," Arthur said wearily.

"Me too, Arthur," Angelina said.

"Jane and I will join up with you later," William responded, also sounding tired. "Hopefully, we can all recuperate enough to do some sightseeing."

They took the rest of the trip easier, sightseeing and making friends. They saw and learnt a lot, inevitably docking back in Barcelona when the cruise was over. They thanked the captain.

"All photos, including wedding photos, will be in the office in three or four days. You will get a chance to choose and buy them."

The taxi took them and their luggage straight home to Angels.

'Mission accomplished,' thought William. 'Four happy people!!'

Chapter 25

The next morning, breakfast and coffee were gratefully received.

Jane spoke first. "It's great to be home, but thank you, Arthur and William. That was a perfect holiday and wedding. Just long enough to keep us totally absorbed. Any longer might have been too long. That was like a heavenly luxury that we will remember forever. Now we have another exciting time. Not the same by a long way, but our exciting grand opening, with the beginning of our business."

"Well, we are ready and up for it," Angelina said. "And did you notice, when you said to the taxi driver "Angels, please," he knew straight away? He did not need directions. We have become a landmark already, despite the new name."

"Arthur," William said. "I hate to remind you, but we are due back at work. Well, actually, we're overdue, but I did warn Arny. Still, it's best if we go tomorrow. I will ring Adrian to arrange him for the day after, but first, today, we need to put the cash from the toolbox in the safe upstairs for now – unless you can think of somewhere better?"

"No, let us do that for now. No time to think of anywhere else. We can do that when we are back. And we had better put the box with the tools back – we will need it."

A few minutes later, William returned after having made a couple of calls. "Adrian will be ready, and I've spoken to the hippies. We will leave after breakfast."

As they were ready to leave, William said, "Bye, girls. We will be back in time for the opening. I have something for you to consider, but it is your business and your choice in the advertising blurb. How about offering 25 per cent or more off for the first 20 people to book? It would allow a lot of people to see how nice it is. Just a thought. Anyway, we had better go."

They were once again sad at leaving.

"It gets harder every time," Arthur said.

"Yes. Sometime soon, we need to arrange something different."

Arny had been busy, and in the extra few days, he had bagged everything for delivery and rearranged the grow rooms, ready for the next harvest in two weeks' time.

"Let us load up and deliver to your brother," William said. "We will call in here for the night before driving back, so see you later."

Arthur left on the motorbike, followed five minutes later by William in the van. The first port of call was the hippy camps. They were providing fifty per cent more, so everyone was happy, including Adrian, who was ready with his cross-country vehicle on the plateau.

"Our wedding made us late. Sorry, Adrian, but I am sure it was worth it. Arny has got the hang of everything."

"Thanks, boys. See you next time!"

They were very soon safely back in the yard. "Hi, Tom, hi, Julian. Is the diesel tank empty?"

"Nearly!"

William handed a roll of notes to Tom. "I will order a refill for you. That is the money for it. I'll give it to you as you are here all the time and will be when they deliver. I will leave it to you two to arrange to share it.

"That is easy," Julian said. "The tank has a dial on, but last time we used about the same.

Both Tom and his wife have diesels, and I have the pickup and diggers, so it works out."

"We might have gone in the morning before you arrive, but we will see you next time and have a better chat then. Goodnight, boys," William said.

He went in and gave Arny a bonus. "That's for the extra work, Arny, thanks. Are you out tonight?"

"Yes, but I won't be late. See you in the morning."

"Yes, for a while, anyway. We are going after breakfast."

On the way back, William and Arthur called in for the last of the liqueurs. Not much else was needed; they just wanted to get home.

"Every time we pull into Angels, it is more impressive," William said.

"Yes, it was the perfect choice," Arthur agreed.

They went in, took the cash upstairs to the safe and then the liqueurs to the girls in the bar.

"Hi, girls. Have you been good?"

"Unfortunately, yes," Angelina answered, laughing.

"We sent circulars round to the local dignitaries to invite them for drinks and a buffet on Friday night," Jane explained. "We ordered some extras and have a chef on trial that we spoke to before. She is eager for a full-time job. We've also got one girl as a waitress for the evening, so along with us four, we should have enough staff to keep everyone entertained."

"Have we enough glasses and plates?" William asked.

"Yes, we have checked everything," Jane said. "Apart from some cooking, we are ready."

"Business cards and leaflets?"

"Yes, all done. Some are on the desk for you to look at, and tomorrow we can collect the pictures of the trip and the wedding. Evidently, they took a few more casual ones; they should be more interesting. Tomorrow, while we are in town, we'll buy a large album; we will need it."

The next morning, Jane and Angelina came back with the pictures. They all gathered round to inspect them. The wedding ones were very professional, the party ones okay and the casual trip ones interesting. Some were strange, but overall, they were pretty good. One problem was that they already needed another album. The photos were packed away as the big day was about to start. People would arrive soon. The cook had finished, so she and the waitress were arranging the buffet on the trestle tables. The drinks, something of everything, were mainly self-service on the other side of the dining room.

"In around an hour, you two girls will need to make a speech," William said.

"Oh, god. I had not thought of that," Jane replied nervously.

"Well, start thinking. It is important for both of you."

The room was filling up. It was getting noisier every minute as more people arrived to chatter.

Jane tapped on the table to quieten people. "Welcome, welcome! We have moved around but have always been in hospitality. From the first time we saw this hotel, we knew we had found our last home: the home and town that we intend to stay in. So besides the intention to create a great business, it is as important, if not more so, to meet you all personally. We would like you all not just as neighbours, but we hope you'll become our friends. Welcome today and welcome anytime!"

"That was my partner, Jane, and I am the other Angel, Angelina," she said, laughing nervously. "We are very alike, and our sentiments are identical. I completely agree with everything she said, and I only need to add that this is totally our business. It was made possible by our husbands, Arthur and William. They also want to integrate into this area and with the people here, which we call home. Please enjoy tonight, and feel free to call in anytime, as we would very much like to see you."

The evening was a success, and friendships were made. Unfortunately, as can happen, some names were forgotten, but most were remembered. Everyone had eaten and drunk their fill. The crowd gradually dwindled. Thanks and good wishes were shared.

By the time they had all gone, the four were tired and ready for bed. The cook and waitress had stayed to clear up, thus cementing themselves in full-time jobs at Angels. They had already been paid, but Arthur felt they deserved extra for showing dedication. He paid them very well on top, and he thanked Maria, the cook, and Tina, the waitress.

"Well, you went above and beyond the call of duty. Goodnight, ladies."

Breakfast was a quiet but happy affair; they were all satisfied.

"Our first guests arrive tomorrow," Jane said. "We have had a lot of inquiries. We should be half-full by the end of the week. We have made a menu with the cook, Maria, but it will take a month to find what to supply. It's going to be a hard learning curve."

"I am sure you will manage," William said reassuringly. "These next few weeks will be the hardest. After that, it will be plain sailing."

By the time the boys had to leave to make their next delivery, the hotel was over half-full. The cook and the dining room had been well and truly tried out, and most jobs had become second nature.

"William, we will have to do the deliveries this time, but it is a long way. How long do you think we can keep it up? It's getting harder. We are getting older, and as long as we are involved, it's dangerous. And if we got caught, we would never be allowed to travel again. The money is good, but do we need it now? Let us go and talk to Adrian and Arny – it will affect them most, after all."

"Bye, girls. We will be back on Tuesday."

"Do you have to keep going?" Jane asked.

"We are trying to sort something out," William said. "We will talk on Tuesday."

"Bye."

William and Arthur left for another boring journey, and as they did, Jane turned to Angelina.

"While they are away, I think I need a pregnancy test."

"That could be awkward, Jane. How sure are you?"

"I am not, but I worry about the possibility. It would put a lot of pressure on you, and do we need that right now?"

"Jane, it would be alright with me. We are secure. If we get busy, we will employ more staff, and on the other hand, it is a lovely thought. We are the best age."

"Well, I will get a test. We might be worrying for nothing."

"Get a test, Jane, and be happy either way. I will be."

Chapter 26

William and Arthur were soon approaching the yard and Arny.

"Hi, Arny. We are a bit earlier, in time to help you trim and bag up. We won't deliver until the day after tomorrow. How is everything with you anyhow?"

"It gets easier every time," Arny said.

"That is good news."

It was nice to have proper chats with Tom and Julian. "All good, William. We both get busier as time goes on."

Delivery came again, and they went in tandem. As usual, Arthur went first, and William was behind with the van. They did the usual collections and moved on to meet with Adrian. After their business, they sat with him, discussing the possibility of a delivery man or if he wished to buy them out lock, stock and barrel.

"We have found it good financially working like this, but having to leave home every few weeks to deliver is hard and takes time. We could deliver at least twice as much at a time, but that means more danger. Anyway, Adrian, put your mind to it and see what you can come up with, please. Meanwhile, we will see you next time!"

They drove back to Arny, wished him well, parked the motorbike and left for home. They did not bother with Andorra this time, too eager to get home as soon as possible.

They were welcomed with open arms. "You are early this time!" Jane said.

"We wanted to get back to you," William said.

"We were watching the television yesterday, and there was an advert for the cruises – quite a long one. Part of it showed our wedding. We all looked good."

"Yes, but it is a worldwide advert. Will it have been shown in the UK? I hope not. That could mean big trouble. You can guarantee they thought they were doing us a favour. Could you see if it will be repeated? Normally they need permission to show anyone on tv. If the wrong person recognises me, I could be in serious trouble."

By the end of the day, the company had promised to withdraw any of the pictures with regret; they understood and were apologetic.

"Let's hope that is the end of it," William said.

After a quick drink on the balcony, it was bedtime.

"We have a phone in our bedroom in case of problems after midnight," William said. "Until then, someone needs to be by the desk."

"How many are booked in at the moment? Do you get disturbed much at night?" Arthur asked.

"Never, so far. Perhaps we have been lucky," Angelina replied.

As they got up in the morning, there was a buzz from the guests having breakfast continually from 6 am until 10. Maria kept everyone happy with their food requests, Tina waited on tables where needed, and she doubled as a cleaner after breakfast. The girls were also doing their bit. All in all, it was a happy ship.

This time as they walked to the town, William was back to his cautious ways, looking for faces that did not fit either as a local or as a holiday-maker. So far, there had been no problems, even when they were approached by a man in the bar who congratulated them on their wedding as he had seen it on the television.

"Where do you live?" William asked.

"I live with a friend. He has lived here for at least ten years. I will only be here another three days; then I have to go back."

"What do you do in the UK?"

"I work in insurance in the city – it pays okay, so I will stay another few years, then perhaps retire out here."

"It's as good as anywhere."

"Perhaps we will see you around. I am Sid, and you are?"

"William, and that over there is Arthur. He married my wife's best friend."

"Not your brother, then?"

"No relation. We have become friends, though."

"Probably see you again before I go back if you are in the harbour here. I come most days."

William made his way over to Arthur, who was buying fresh fish that had just landed on the dock.

"It does not get fresher than this, William," he said. "What do you think?"

"Buy it. If the customers don't eat it, we will. You could ring Angelina to see if they need anything to make the sauce. We could get it on the way back if they need it."

"No, they have everything, but they did say to buy a few more as Maria will make fish specials for tomorrow. They are one of her specialities."

"How many? A dozen, do you think?"

"That should do. After all, they land some every day if we want to come down for more."

They carried it in. "Is a dozen enough for you, Maria?"

"Yes, that is enough. You might have to eat some, but it should all sell."

When they got back to the hotel, the girls were in the dining room checking and entertaining the customers, all looking happy. Arthur and William left them to it and took beers out onto their private balcony.

"This is the life, William. I just hope Adrian comes up with a plan to buy or something. He can have a private mortgage if he likes."

"Why not? Or, if he prefers, rent the house and equipment for a fair price; then, if they got found out, they could disappear, losing just the business. No one would lose the house as we would just deny any knowledge of the goings on inside. I think that is the best for everyone, don't you? Call him tomorrow. You will have to be very cryptic, but Adrian is very bright and will soon catch on."

"Yes, I will put it to him. Then he can have time to consider it before we meet with the next delivery."

There were still quite a lot of guests in the dining hall, along with some casual diners. None looked ready to move; they were being far too well looked after and not wanting the evening to end too soon.

"Jane, my love, you are suffering from your own success. Do we complain or cheer?"

"We will get tired, but at the moment, Angelina and I are very happy and loving it!!"

"Another late night, then,"

"Afraid so, William, but go to bed. I will join you later."

"No, I can wait for my lovely wife, and I know Arthur will wait. Perhaps the two of us should learn to play chess."

"We will arrange two afternoons a week off and a full day for all of us together and see how it goes."

"Well, that is a lot better, so good."

These routines made a difference, and everyone was happy. The boys had found their places helping with hotel duties, fetching and carrying from stores and selecting fish at the harbour. They were feeling more relaxed every day. They had made a few friends in town that they always stopped to speak to.

Chapter 27

Early one such morning, they stopped to talk, as usual, and sat in the sun.

"William, I will go and buy the fish. I won't be long."

"Okay, Arthur. Take your time; we are early yet."

Arthur wandered on. William watched him disappear round the corner when he suddenly felt a blow to the back and a sharp pain in his chest.

The man who was now next to him put his arm on his shoulder and whispered in his ear, "You are done, William. At last, you are done. There is no escaping this skinny knife; that's professional."

Another man put a piece of paper in his hand. William started to cough and choke. He fell back in his seat, blood coming from his mouth. The men walked away, and one took a picture with his phone.

William was alone when Arthur came back. Shocked, he ran to get the car and lifted William in. Throwing the fish aside, he drove straight to the hospital door and called for assistance. William was carried in instantly. Arthur took the paper William was still holding. Written on the now very bloodstained paper was WILLIAM PAID IN FULL. Arthur knew immediately what it meant. He rang Jane to come to the hospital as quickly as she could. Both ladies were there in a minute.

"What has happened?" Jane screamed. "Where is he?" She didn't wait for answers and found the room where he was being frantically worked on, all to no avail.

They went in for William's last moments.

"Arthur," William croaked.

Arthur leaned close and could just hear William's words.

"They got me. It's over. Please do nothing. Look after Jane. Promise me, Arthur. Do nothing."

"I promise, William." It was not what Arthur wanted, but there was nothing to be gained. He knew that, for the good of the rest of them, he had to let it go!

A couple of times, William managed to say, "I love you, Janey."

She was screaming, "I love you, William. Don't leave me!"

But it was out of his hands. He died.

With a lot of help, they managed to tear Jane away and back to Angels, where she collapsed in their room. She froze mentally and physically. She could not sleep. She never really tried; it would have been hopeless. Night came, and the bed was empty without him. She was saying over and over, "My life is finished. I can face nothing without him."

In the morning, she got up quietly, let herself out of the back door, got into the car and drove off before the others knew. She had gone several miles along the coast when she remembered there was a cliff top overhanging the sea. She stopped the car facing the edge to say her farewells, hoping William could somehow hear her; any miracle gratefully accepted. She finished all she could bear to say. As she gripped the wheel, engine revving, she heard a message arrive on her phone. She was tempted to ignore it, but perhaps it was a miracle, and it was William. It was not the miracle she was hoping for, but a different one.

It read, "The results of your pregnancy test came back positive. You are nearly 3 months pregnant. Please ring for an appointment as soon as possible."

Jane screamed, "William!" several times and cried helplessly. Her mind hurt as though about to explode. She drove slowly, as if in a dream, back to Angels.

Angelina came running out. "Jane, love. Jane, come in, please. Arthur is out looking for you. Where have you been?"

Jane held out her phone for Angelina to read. "William saved me again, Angelina, just in time. How does he do it? I will have a little William or Willomina. I don't care which. It will be his and the most loved and cared for child ever."

Arthur arrived back and put his arms around Jane. Angelina showed him Jane's phone with the text message still displayed on the screen.

"Jane," Arthur said, "I don't blame you. I have felt the same! For me, Angelina is my saviour, and the baby is yours. One day, I will tell you how William saved me from a living hell, and we have hardly been apart since. He got into a hopeless situation but never complained. He fought it off several times, but something had to happen, I suppose. All the while, he protected me from it. I owe him everything. There are men everywhere in awe of him, as you will see. This weekend, if Angelina can spare you, I will take you to work to see absolutely everything. You will be in his shoes. He was, well, we were retiring this week to stay at Angels."

"We can manage here. Please go with him, Jane."

As they drove out, Arthur started the story, and by the time they drove into the yard, he had finished telling it, warts and all, finishing with, "A bit naughty, but a real gentleman with immense guts." They got out of the car and crossed the yard.

"You know Tom and Julian, of course," Arthur said as they came over to greet them.

"Yes," Jane said.

"We loved the guy," Tom said. "He put us both on our feet. There was and is nothing we would not do for these two gentlemen without question. And if there is ever anything we can do for you, please don't hesitate to ask."

The sincerity was there in their eyes, along with a tear or two. Arthur took her inside to see the grow rooms. She was not phased or shocked but was clearly impressed.

"This is Arny; he now runs this production. Smart and loyal, he is Adrian's brother. It will now be under new management with his brother, who you met in Andorra and who we will deliver to in a couple of hours."

They loaded up and also put the motorbike in the van. Next were the collections from the hippy camps, and an hour after that, they delivered to Adrian on the plateau.

He was visibly upset. "I don't know what to say. I have never met such decent, honourable men like these two, and now one is gone, never to be forgotten. I will pay the new rent in cash every month, as agreed, hoping that will bring you to Andorra often. Please keep in touch. I am lost for words."

"We have something to look forward to, don't we, Jane?" Arthur prompted.

"Yes, I am pregnant. Thank the lord for that anyway. We will see you when we come to Andorra shopping."

They waved goodbye and drove home to Angels. "I hope you are glad to have come to see everything," Arthur said.

"Yes, and thank you for the story. Upsetting though it all was, I am grateful. I needed it, and in the future, there will be no questions left unanswered."

The next year was a blur and passed easily. The wills had been read and explained, including the banks and lock boxes. Even without her share of Angels, Jane was a relatively wealthy woman. She loved working there with her best friends, and they were a very willing family for little now two-year-old Willomina: an energetic and inquisitive girl. Every time Jane looked at her, her thoughts were the same. 'You, my William, will never want for anything.'

"Mummy, what was my daddy like?"

"'Mina, sweetheart. Go upstairs to the big mirror. Stand in front of it, smile a lot, and you will see him. He was just like you. Aren't you lucky?"

"Yes, Mummy."